Night Wind

The big-bodied bear had covered almost half of the three-quarter mile distance to the substation feeder road when he stopped to examine his prize. The screams that had a first infuriated him were now just an occasional moan as the little girl's blood loss from the teeth marks in her right shoulder caused her to mercifully drift in and out of consciousness.

He wasn't really hungry since the DNA sample pen was always full of corn, but his natural instinct had taken over when this small human had trespassed on his turf while he was raiding the garbage.

Now he watched her for about two minutes and then rolled her over with a swat of his large paw. A small moan escaped her lips as the ribs that had been broken in the initial attack shot sharp pains throughout her body, and the bear backed up slightly.

ISBN 978-0-9862487-1-9

Published by Purple Sage Entertainment, Odessa, Texas

All characters, events, and conspiracies in this book are fictitious. Any similarity to real persons, living or dead, and any real or imagined conspiracy is coincidental, and not intended by the author. Product names used herein are not an endorsement of this work by the product name owners.

Printed in the United States of America on acid-free paper.

Contact: will@purplesageentertainment.com

W.W.Brock
brock@wwbrock.com
http://www.wwbrock.com

NIGHT WIND

by

W.W. Brock

W.W. Brock

Dedication

I would like to dedicate this book to my wife, the love of my life. Without her support and encouragement, I would not have started writing.

CHAPTER 1

"I will also send wild beasts among you, which shall rob you of your children, and destroy your cattle, and make you few in number; and your highways shall be desolate," (Leviticus 26:22)

Earl Johnson's widow, Naomi, stood weeping silently by the graveside as the pastor gave his final benediction to Earl's remains, that is he would have if there had been any remains. Earl had quite simply disappeared into the swamp with only a trace amount of his blood found in the boat when a Department of Natural Resources Officer, Lieutenant Michael Tucker located it not far from the Punch Bowl landing on the Little Pee Dee River. After a massive search of the area was called off two weeks later, Earl was declared missing and presumed dead, which led to an empty coffin being buried at his memorial.

"Lord, we commit our brother's remains to you and ask that you be with his wife and children in this dark hour of their lives, Amen," the pastor finished, and the gathering of family and friends closed around Naomi and six of the nine children that Earl had left behind.

They had almost no income from their family business, which had failed in the years previous due to the collapsed economy, and Earl had been their only support.

Michael Tucker waited until the red-haired reporter from WLIB and most of the other mourners had cleared out, before he and his wife Hanna, large with their first child, drew near to Naomi and expressed their condolences. Tuck had taken up a collection from the community of fishermen and hunters that had enjoyed Earl's friendship and comedic antics all of the years past, and now he quietly slipped an envelope containing twenty-five hundred dollars into the grieving widow's hand.

"From Earl's friends," was all that he could say without his voice breaking, and Naomi just nodded her appreciation as Hanna slipped her arms around the older woman to comfort her. Life was going to get much harder for the Johnson family without Earl, but Tuck felt that they were strong enough to make it, especially with the support of their close-knit family, and Earl's friends.

"Michael," Hanna spoke softly as they were walking back to the car after the graveside service, "I've been watching you ever since Earl went missing, and it seems like you are holding a lot in. Can you talk to me about it?"

"I'm okay, Love. It's just that since we found out that some of our own people were involved in bringing those cats in here, I've been having second thoughts about this job. I can't help but feel like the government owes Johnny Faraday, Charlene Simmons, and Max Allen's Father a whole lot more than a small settlement for their being 'inconvenienced' by that cougar attacking them. This thing with Earl disappearing has been bothering me a lot also. Earl was an experienced hunter and fisherman. He knew the swamp like the back of his hand and practically lived down there. I am having a hard time believing that he fell overboard and drowned, which is the official story," Tuck was really wound up and once the dam broke, he let everything out, "I think that the other cougar is involved, and, somehow, I am going to hunt that animal down, with or without the blessing of Colonel McNeery, and the cougar is not the only thing that I am going to go after."

Hanna knew better than to argue with her husband when he was this upset so she just gave his hand a soft squeeze and followed him back to the car.

"Daddy has a surprise for you when we get down there this afternoon," She said in a casual sort of way that made Tuck immediately suspicious.

"What kind of surprise, Hon?" he asked with just a little anxiety in his voice. Tuck was very aware of the fact that the

Albright clan all had a penchant for practical jokes and surprises that often left the recipient red faced and speechless.

"Oh, the kind of surprise where we get to eat at a really nice place instead of one of your greasy spoons for a change," she answered with a big grin. "Daddy is taking us to RIOZ Brazilian Steakhouse for a big celebration tonight!"

"Wow, what is he celebrating?" Tuck was all in for RIOZ, and his excitement was starting to show.

"That I can't tell you, Michael, you will just have to be patient. You know that thing that you want to learn on your own and not be taught? Practice that," Hanna replied with a laugh. Her father was always telling Tuck the same thing because it was the one area where he was still like a little boy.

Their solitude was broken by a shout from the road where they had parked their car, "Lieutenant Tucker, Lieutenant Tucker...may I have a word with you?" Tuck looked up to see the lady reporter from WLIB News walking in their direction with her cameraman following.

"Not now ma'am, my wife is feeling faint and I need to get her home!" he leaned over to Hanna who was looking at him with surprise and said, "Try to look faint, hurry!"

It was too late; the reporter was now in their path with an 'I'm not leaving until we talk' looking on her face.

"Lieutenant Tucker, you have been avoiding me since we broke that story about the cougar conspiracy. Why?"

"Because I work for the DNR, and it is their policy that all interaction with the media comes from within the DNR public relations department. If you have questions, you need to talk to them. Would you like a contact number?" Tuck asked, just hoping that she would go away.

"No, I don't want their number! I want you to give me an honest answer to one question. You owe me that much after I put my job on the line for you guys over the cougar conspiracy story.

WLIB is under pressure to find a way to fire me for breaking a story that caused embarrassment to the government, so just one question, please," The red-haired reporter seemed almost on the verge of tears, and before Tuck could decline, Hanna spoke up, "Michael will talk to you, Maggie, but just keep it short, my feet are swelling up, and I really need to get home."

Hanna had gone to high school with Margaret O'Brien and had never liked her or her cheerleading pals who always seemed so pretentious, but today she felt sorry for the young woman and attributed it to the hormones from the baby.

Maggie looked at Hanna with surprise then said, "Thanks, Hanna, I appreciate you intervening with your husband for me. I won't keep you very long. Here is my question: Officer Tucker, do you think that Earl Johnson's disappearance is related to the cougars that were reported to be still in the area? If so, what is the next action that the DNR is going to take?"

"That was two questions Maggie, which one would you like for me to answer?" Tuck responded without a smile. Hanna gave him a nudge with her elbow; which meant, "Act human!"

"I'm sorry Maggie," Tuck responded to the elbow, then, "The answer to your first question is that Earl Johnson could have just fallen overboard, hit his head, and drowned, or Earl could have been bitten by a snake and drowned, or Earl could have been dragged into the water by an alligator. It would be a very long shot guess, and kind of irresponsible to say that a cougar did this without any evidence to back up the statement. The truth is that now that the cougar is here, and by here, I mean within a hundred miles of Conway, South Carolina, it has every right to exist in the environment as its ancestors did for hundreds of years. That should answer your questions."

"Thank you, Lieutenant Tucker," Maggie O'Brien signaled the cameraman to kill the mike and the camera. When she knew that they were not recording, she said to Tuck and Hanna, "I can't even imagine what you both have been through. If you need anything that I can help you with, please call me," she then turned to Hanna, "I wish that I had known you better in school, Hanna. Can we get together over lunch sometime and talk?"

Hanna hesitated until she felt the gentle nudge of Tuck's elbow in her back, "I would love to Maggie. Just give me a call."

The two women hugged as if they were old friends, and then Maggie O'Brien shook Tuck's hand before turning away to give the cameraman some directions.

Hanna dug her elbow into Tuck's side in a not so gentle way, "Thanks, you big dope, I didn't want to meet her for lunch, and you knew that!"

"Well, I didn't want to answer her questions either but that didn't seem to stop you now did it?" Tuck answered with a big grin, "Let's get home and change before we go to Harry's. I am dying to find out what this celebration is all about."

What they did not see was the nondescript, tan Chevrolet that had a handheld directional microphone pointed at them while they were talking to Margaret O'Brien.

"Follow them at a distance, he will want to know what this celebration is about also," the man with the listening device told the driver of the car.

A funny thing about instincts, lower order animals live by them and most humans are afraid to follow them, not so with Michael Tucker! Tuck felt like someone was trying to kill him from the first time that he set his feet in Iraq. His instincts for survival kept him alive on several occasions and were honed to a razor edge by the time that he left Afghanistan for the last time after two years in that dark part of hell. Since the attack on Tuck, Hanna, and their family and friends, he rarely went anywhere without that built in radar taking in all of his surroundings, sometimes unconsciously.

The first time that the tan Chevrolet came into his peripheral view on the way home after the funeral, Tuck dismissed his first thought that they were being followed as an overreaction to the events that they had survived just a short time before. When the same car showed up six back in the line of cars behind them on the way down Highway 501 to Myrtle Beach, Tuck's mind went into overdrive, running scenarios that would put Hanna and him in the clear if they were attacked.

With his eyes darting to the review mirror as often as possible, Tuck picked his cell phone off the seat and punched the speed dial for his friend, Sheriff's Deputy Isaac Baumgarner. "Ike, Tuck here. What's your twenty?"

"Hey Tuck," came the jovial response. The two men had grown close during the two years that Tuck had been with the DNR, "I'm serving some papers on a fellow down here in Carolina Forest for baiting bears, what's up?"

"Ike, Hanna and I are on the way to Harry's. I'm just passing the hospital on 501, and I think the tan Chevy six cars back is tailing us. Can you slow them down a bit for me?" Tuck explained the situation.

"Tuck my boy; this is what I live for! Hold the speed limit until I get in position, then speed up so I can write a big ticket when they try to keep up," Ike replied, "I'll give you a call as soon as I have some ID on these guys."

"Thanks, Ike, but be careful," Tuck hung up the phone.

Hanna looked at him with big eyes through the conversation but didn't say anything until he put the phone down.

"Michael, Are you sure that we are being followed? Is this starting up all over again?" she asked in a worried voice.

"Hanna, I don't think it ever stopped entirely. People with the power to do the things that we uncovered rarely quit, they just pull back a little bit when they get caught. I don't think we have anything to worry about yet, but we will be extra careful won't *we*?" Tuck responded with an emphasis on the 'we'.

Hanna started to respond but was interrupted by the phone.

"Go ahead Ike, are you ready?" Tuck asked.

"Take it up to seventy Tuck. I've got a buddy of mine sitting up ahead that will shake them down for you," Ike sounded as if he were laughing at the prospect of whatever might happen to the people in the Chevy.

"Thanks, Ike, I owe you. How about meeting for lunch tomorrow?" Tuck asked while he sped the car up to seventy miles an hour.

"That's a big ten-four on the lunch Tuck, but you don't owe me anything. This is for Earl Johnson!" Tuck heard the anger in his voice as Ike hung the phone up.

As Tuck and Hanna came through the green light at the intersection at Carolina Forest, they saw the front of a State Trooper's unmarked car sitting in one of the small businesses back off the road. The Chevrolet had pulled into the left-hand lane in an attempt to keep pace with Tuck and lost the advantage of being able to hide in traffic. They also did not see the big Dodge of the Trooper until it was barreling up behind them with the blue lights on, signaling them to pull over.

They were almost at Harry's house when Ike called again, "Tuck, those fellows were FBI, and they were some kind of pissed!" Ike said with a laugh, "That didn't stop my buddy from writing a ticket, though. He felt like they should be detained for a while for all of the cussin' that they were doing."

"Thanks, Ike, we'll keep our eyes open. I wonder what they wanted anyway?" Tuck asked with a puzzled tone in his voice.

"I would imagine that they are a little irritated with you for showing them up to be a bunch of untrustworthy snakes. I've got to get back to work, see you tomorrow for lunch," Ike ended the call.

"Well, what did he say?" Hanna's impatience was showing.

"FBI, Hon, nothing to worry about," Tuck replied, but he had that old feeling that something bad was about to happen.

CHAPTER 2

Tuck didn't recognize the car that was in Harry Albright's driveway when they pulled up but noted that it was a rental. "Were you expecting some visitors from out of town, Babe?" he said as he pulled into the lawn to keep from blocking the other car in.

"I don't think so, but you know Daddy, he is kind of secretive when he wants to be," Hanna responded with a smile, "Let's go in, and solve the mystery."

Harry Albright met them at the door and gave them each a big hug, then said, "Tuck, have I got a surprise for you!" and led them into the kitchen where Bob Pike was standing with a big grin on his face.

"Bob, what in the world are you doing here, I thought you were in Honduras?" Tuck blurted out in surprise as they shook hands and slapped each other on the back.

"Well," Bob replied, "we needed to raise some money for the ministry down there, and I was elected to come back for a few speaking engagements. Abby stayed behind on this trip but sent her love. It certainly is good to see you folks again, Tuck."

After hugging Bob, Hanna joined her stepmother, Kathryn, while Harry motioned for Tuck and Bob to follow him to the porch. "While the ladies are finishing getting ready, let's talk about anything unusual that any of us might have seen or heard in the last few months. I'll start with hearing that Special Agent Morris was quietly and quickly transferred about a month after our last meeting with him. I haven't been in touch with the new guy, but I understand that he is a DOJ pick, and has a reputation for being somewhat cold toward anyone not directly on board with the administration's new policies...anybody else?"

"Well, Abby and I have been under surveillance since we arrived in Honduras. At first, we just thought that it might be their government keeping tabs on newcomers. Now I'm not so sure," Bob added to the conversation.

"Hanna and I were followed from the cemetery today, and the same car was behind us on the way down here tonight. Ike arranged for them to be delayed, and they showed FBI identification. If they are involved, I would bet the bank that we are being monitored in our calls, emails, and contacts, although I can't think of a good reason for that," Tuck said while winking at the two other men.

All three had their backs to the street and were muffling their voices as much as possible, just in case someone was listening.

"I think that we should just act like nothing is amiss and keep our regular schedules," Harry said quietly, "starting with getting our behinds to RIOZ for a fabulous meal. That way the girls will not have any more stress heaped on their plates unless the activity heats up a bit. Are we in agreement?"

Both Bob and Tuck responded with a hearty, "Yes Sir!" as Hanna and Kathryn came out of the house.

Once they were seated at RIOZ and their orders were taken, Hanna made an announcement, "I want to thank Daddy for this night and the opportunity to surprise my husband with a good report. As you all know, I went in for my checkup and ultrasound yesterday and both the baby and I are doing fine. What some of you may not know," she looked straight at Tuck and squeezed his hand, "is that we are having a baby boy!"

Tuck looked like his face was going to break in half with the big grin that appeared, "Honey, that is wonderful, but why didn't you tell me last night?"

"The doctor wanted to make absolutely sure before we said anything because she knew how much you wanted a son, Michael Tucker, Jr., so she called me this morning just before we left for the funeral with the news. I told you that there was a surprise!"

Hanna was almost jumping out of her seat with glee as she saw the excitement spread across her husband's face.

The next hour was like a blur to Tuck. First Bob had shown up unexpectedly, and then Hanna broke her news. He was so caught up in the moment that the couple two tables over that seemed to be observing them every time that Tuck glanced in their direction almost slipped past his radar. Toward the end of the meal, the manager of RIOZ, and good friend of Harry Albright, Henrique, stopped by the table to check on his guests. After the pleasantries were exchanged, Tuck caught his attention, and as Henrique leaned in to hear over the bustling sounds of the busy restaurant, Tuck whispered something into his ear.

"Absolutely my friend," Henrique exclaimed, "it would be a pleasure!"

"What did you say to him, Honey?" Hanna asked.

"I asked for a doggie bag," Tuck responded with a big grin.

As they were leaving, Henrique came to the front of the restaurant and presented Tuck with a brown paper sack with the RIOZ logo on the front.

"Obrigado, my friend!" Henrique said in his gracious Brazilian style as he passed the bag over.

"Michael Tucker, I can't believe that you asked for a doggie bag from a Brazilian Churrascaria!" Hanna said in embarrassment as they walked to the car.

"Relax everybody," Tuck defended himself, "I asked Henrique for the drink glasses from the table where the couple sat checking us out all night. Since it is better to be safe than sorry, I'll get these off to the lab in the morning and see if we were being watched by curious tourists or something more sinister."

"Who do we have that you can trust, Tuck?" Bob asked, sounding a bit dubious, "I thought that we had used up all of our aces in the hole long ago."

"I think that we should be careful about what we talk about and where we talk until I get these analyzed, Bob. Let's meet in the morning for breakfast and catch up on everything. We can talk then," Tuck replied in a cautious tone.

He knew as well as Bob Pike that even their cell phones could be broadcasting the conversations within the car, and there was the possibility that if they were being followed, the car might be bugged also.

Tuck and Hanna said goodnight to the Albrights and to Bob when they returned to Harry's home. Bob Pike would be spending the next several nights with Harry and Kathryn as their guest, but promised to get up to Conway to spend time with Tuck and say hello to all of the fellows that congregated for breakfast before making their individual rounds.

The ride home was filled with conversation about the son that Tuck and Hanna were expecting, and for the forty minutes that it took, it seemed as if nothing else existed except their happiness at this precious moment, which was rudely interrupted when Tuck's cell phone starting ringing incessantly.

"Hello, Lieutenant Tucker speaking," Tuck answered the phone. The voice on the other end belonged to one of the two new DNR officers, Privates Joel Biggs and Patrick (Junior) Knowles that had been brought into the area after Bob Pike had retired, and while Tuck was on leave. Biggs was older than Tuck by several years and had been a county sheriff's deputy upstate before joining the DNR a year before while Knowles was in his early twenties and new to the force.

"Lieutenant, this is Private Biggs, I hate to bother you this late, but one of the fellows that have been coyote hunting up above Punch Bowl has something that you should see," Joel Biggs sounded as if he were out of breath.

"Joel, it is almost nine o'clock, can't this wait until morning?" Tuck asked as he saw the disgusted look on Hanna's face.

"I don't think so sir. You are going to want to see what he found as soon as possible!" Private Biggs was insistent, "It's an old blue and black shoe sir, but he says that there are some bones close by that looked human!"

"What is your location Joel, and who have you called in?" Tuck's mind was in high gear as he took charge of the situation.

"I've got the sheriff's department coming now and a forensics team, just in case," Biggs replied, "We are about halfway down Punch Bowl road on that dirt road that turns off to the left now, but I can wait until you get here if you want."

"No, it will take me a while. I've got to get home and change so start your search but be very careful not to let anyone mess up the area just in case there are tracks that we can follow," Tuck ordered.

"Yes sir, I understand," Biggs responded. Tuck had confidence in the man's ability to control the scene as well as in his hunting skills. If there were any animals involved in whatever the hunter had found, then Biggs would probably be the best man for the job.

"And Joel, be very careful, understand?" "Yes sir!" and the call ended.

"What is it, Michael?" Hanna asked with a worried tone in her voice.

"I think that they might have found Earl," Tuck whispered.

CHAPTER 3

The female cougar and her three spotted kittens, one female and two males, had left the shelter of the old tobacco barn in the week following Earl Johnson's killing because of the increased presence of men in the woods. She had moved up the Little Pee Dee River bottom almost two miles to a remote part of the cypress swamp where it seemed unlikely that they would be found. The kittens were still small, about the size of small bobcats, and relied on their mother to furnish the meat that they needed to survive.

Except where her kittens were concerned, the female had almost no fear of man and considered them no different that the deer and pigs that she killed when an opportunity was presented. Earl Johnson had been no exception. Tonight she stalked a yearling buck that was meandering along the much-used game trail that passed in front of her position. The buck was within twenty feet of the big female cat when she sprang from ambush, and it tried to escape with a leap away from the cougar. By the second ground-eating pounce, the cougar had overtaken the hapless young whitetail and fastened her teeth into the back of his neck as her razor sharp claws secured a death hold on his body. Soon his struggles seized and the big cat relaxed her grip long enough to signal to her cubs with a whistle, that dinner was served.

The three kittens leaped upon the still quivering body of the deer with savage ferocity in an effort to mimic their mother who had ripped the abdomen open with a tug of a scalpel-like claw. The kittens fought over the heart as the mother pulled it still beating from the deer before she turned back to the task of feeding herself on the soft organs and then tearing into the muscle tissue of the dying animal. Like the huge male that she had mated with, her needs were for about twenty pounds of meat a day and more with the kittens still suckling her.

A slight movement in the surrounding scrub brush caught the cat's attention and she instantly froze in position, every muscle taught as a coiled spring for the possibility of an attack against her and her kittens. Standing twenty feet away, just barely noticeable in the brush was a large coyote, glaring at her with his head down and teeth bared. Coyotes were a problem for the cougar. They seemed to materialize like ghosts when she was fortunate to kill, and tonight was no exception. A low growl came from her throat as she moved slowly toward the coyote that held his ground against the advance of the larger and more deadly foe. The kittens growled and spit much like an ordinary house cat would in the presence of a dog but stayed close to the deer carcass.

As the distance between the two decreased, the cat suddenly sprung toward the coyote that just as suddenly disappeared into the scrub. In the split second that followed, two more coyotes rushed the kittens and seized the female and one male in their razor sharp teeth, shaking them violently to break their backs before running off into the swamp. The big cat wheeled around and sprang back to the defense of her kittens, but it was too late. The surviving male was spitting and hissing at the coyotes that were just out of sight in the brush, but very much intent on gaining the deer carcass from the cougar. She reached the surviving kitten and grabbed him by the scruff of his neck before bounding into the woods and away from the coyotes, and the bodies of her offspring. Grief for her kittens would have to wait. It was imperative that the cat find a safe haven for herself and the last kitten.

It was late when Tuck reached the area where the hunter had found the shoe. Private Biggs was waiting for him with a light waving in his hand. They had been on two-way radio since Tuck had left the house since there was almost no cell phone service in this remote area. Several sheriffs' deputies were on the scene along with the hunter and a forensics team that was working in the dark trying to gather more evidence.

"Good evening, Lieutenant," Biggs greeted Tuck cordially, "The men are up ahead about a hundred yards. We've got an old collapsed barn that appears to have been a den of sorts. There doesn't seem to be anything in it now, though."

Tuck liked Joel Biggs, but he believed very strongly in the military tradition that 'familiarity breeds contempt' so he treated him with respect, but as a subordinate, "Hello, Private. Let's see if the sheriff's department is going to stay on this all night."

The two men walked through the pines to the small clearing where the collapsed barn was located. One of the deputies, the young man that Tuck had seen at Millie Frakes greeted them as they walked up.

"Hello, Lieutenant Tucker. We've got just about all of the bone fragments that we can find here tonight bagged. Unless you want something else done tonight, I think that we will secure the area until first light," Deputy Trip said to Tuck.

"I'd like to see the shoe that was found. I know what Earl was wearing when he disappeared," Tuck said quietly to the deputy.

"Yes sir, I'll have one of the fellows bring it over," he said as he turned momentarily to give an order to one of the forensics team, "I hope that it is Earl's in a way. Don't get me wrong, I just think that Naomi needs the closure that this could bring."

Tuck agreed and was about to say so when one of the other deputies handed him a plastic evidence bag with the remains of the shoe. With his flashlight shining through the plastic of the bag, Tuck could see that the shoe was a match for the ones that Earl had been wearing. The memory brought a lump to Tuck's throat and a tear to his eye.

Suddenly the semi-stillness of the evening was broken by a long high-pitched scream that sounded as if it were coming from somewhere in the river bottoms. The hair on Tuck's arms and the nape of his neck stood straight up as he heard the haunting scream of a female cougar, a scream that seemed to be filled with rage and hatred.

Tuck turned to Joel Biggs who was shining a light in the direction of the sound. All of the other men were frozen in fear, their wide eyes peering into the darkness beyond their lights for any sign of the terror that was wailing like a banshee.

"Biggs, let's wrap this up and get these people out of here. When you come back in the morning, I'd advise bringing a shotgun loaded with 4/0 buck. Wear your leggings also, you and I are going hunting!"

"Yes, sir!" Private Biggs responded as he turned to the other men, "Okay men, we need to wrap this up and get out of here for tonight," and he walked off to help get the gear loaded back onto the four wheelers that they had packed it in on.

Tuck pulled the big Ruger P-90 .45ACP from its holster and flashed the NiteSiter illumination dots on his sights with the LED light that he was carrying. The dots would stay visible for a couple of hours and give him an edge just in case he encountered the cougar on the way back to the truck. He wouldn't make the mistake of not having his Remington 870 in his hand when he came back in the morning!

CHAPTER 4

The female cougar had climbed high into the large limbs of an old live oak tree, carrying the male kitten by the nape of his neck. After several hours, the yipping cry of the pack moved back downstream on the Little Pee Dee, and the cougar, driven by hunger and loss, decided to make a midnight hunt near a human habitation. With a low growl to let the kitten know not to follow, she jumped to the ground and started at a run toward the Old Pee Dee highway where several small farms were located. Here she would take whatever hapless animal or person crossed her path.

Cyrus Bean, a man in his mid-seventies still powerfully built from the years of hard work in the local sawmilling operation, woke from a fitful sleep for his almost hourly trip to the bathroom. His prostate had been bothering him for years, but despite the best advice from his family doctor, Cyrus decided to ignore the problem and put up with the aggravation of waking every hour or so to go to the bathroom. Cyrus' small, secluded homestead was located on the edge of the Little Pee Dee Swamp where the only night sounds were the tree frogs chirping when the weather was warm. He and his wife, Sarah, had raised two sons here, and she was buried beneath the old live oak that stood on the back of the large lot, just behind the garden that had been their mainstay for food through many difficult years.

As was his habit lately, Cyrus donned an old pair of bib overalls after his trip to the bathroom and started out of the back door to visit Sarah's grave for a few minutes before he went back to bed. The night air was cool to the skin on his arms and shoulders, and the dew on the grass felt good to his old and tired bare feet.

"Sarah would fuss at me for not putting on my shirt and shoes," He thought with a smile as a small tear leaked its way out of his right eye at the thought. He hastily brushed it away with the back of one of his gnarled hands as the gravestone showed up in the light of his small flashlight.

"Hello, my love," Cyrus proclaimed softly as he knelt beside the grave, his right hand reaching for the tombstone to steady himself a bit as the stiff old knees came in contact with the ground.

As the big cougar launched herself in a ferocious attack that killed Cyrus instantly when her teeth penetrated the back of his skull at the cervical vertebrate; his last thoughts on this earth where the ones of love for his departed wife.

Desperate to feed, she satiated her hunger immediately so her kitten could nurse when she returned. Tomorrow she would find another den that would ensure his safety while she hunted.

"Michael, is that you?" came Hanna's sleepy voice from the bedroom.

"Yes Love, go back to sleep, it's after eleven and I have to get up at three thirty," Michael replied.

He made short work of hanging his clothes on the back of a kitchen chair to be ready for the morning, then took his snake boots from the hall closet and set them by the bed along with two 'burner' phones that he had picked up earlier in the day. After writing a short note to Hanna with instructions on using the phone, Tuck quietly joined his sleeping wife for the short few hours that he would get to sleep.

Three thirty came too early for Tuck's sleep deprived mind. He had a hard time falling asleep, and when it finally did come, the dreams that came with it left him tired. The one reoccurring dream was of the big cat charging him, and the shotgun trigger being impossible to pull. He woke for the fourth or fifth time, wet with sweat, and smelled the coffee brewing in the kitchen, but by four o'clock Tuck had showered, dressed and was pulling the truck out of the drive and heading for his rendezvous with Private Biggs. Maybe today would put the cat problems firmly in the past so he could concentrate on finding out who was responsible for the tail that had been put on them, and why they were still being followed.

He pulled into the power line right-of-way off Punch Bowl Road and parked behind Biggs' truck. Joel Biggs was already out and sitting on the tailgate with his Remington 870 propped up beside him. Tuck gave him a wave and a smile and then unloaded his daypack and rifle from the truck.

"Good morning, Lieutenant," Biggs greeted him in a quiet voice, "What is the plan?"

"Good morning Joel. I thought we would move down the power line and see if there might be some signs along one of the game trails that we could follow. From what Henry Albright told me, the cougar tracks will be almost impossible to see unless we have a good deal of luck, so stay sharp," Tuck responded.

Each man took a side of the power line, separated by a distance of about one hundred yards, and they both studied the grass and brush that marked the edges of the right-of- way for the telltale signs of a game trail. By nine o'clock they had covered almost a quarter of a mile of the power line when Tuck saw a familiar clump of fur that had been caught in a cat-vine growing over a much-used trail. He quickly signaled for Biggs and pulled a piece of safety orange ribbon from his jacket pocket to mark the find.

"Is that what I think it is, Lieutenant?" Biggs asked while kneeling down to exam the ground around the trail.

"Well, if you are thinking that this fur belongs to a cougar, then it probably is," Tuck replied with a chuckle, "We need to get over where you were and see if there is anything that will give us a direction that she was traveling in, although I'm not going to get my hopes up."

Another hour passed by and neither man had found anything resembling a paw print made by a cougar when suddenly a faint breeze brought the unmistakable smell of cat scat to Tuck's nose.

"Joel, can you smell that?" Tuck called to his helper excitedly, "Cat crap!"

"I smell it too, Lieutenant. It seems to be coming from that direction," as he motioned toward the river bottom.

Now they moved quickly and quietly with all of their senses on alert. Biggs saw the pile of leaves first and noted that they looked as if they had just been raked up. Tuck picked up a stick and pulled the leaves off the aromatic pile, then pulled his compass out and noted the direction that the cat appeared to be heading.

"Joel, I want to get some men out here to help in the hunt before we go in there after that cat. I have to meet with Deputy Baumgarner in about an hour and will have him send out the word. You get a fix on this location with your GPS and make a stand over on the other side from about five o'clock until dark. Did you pack a rifle in the truck?" Tuck said as he outlined his plan.

"No sir, I just brought the shotgun and my Glock," was the response.

"My .308 is in the truck. Use that and I will pick it up from you in the morning," Tuck replied as they walked back toward the vehicles, "As a matter of fact, you can sit in your truck with it if you can make that five hundred yard shot down to the ribbon."

Biggs gave him a big grin and then replied confidently, "We both had the same training, sir. That is an easy shot with your rifle!"

Tuck left Biggs admiring his gun and preparing for the afternoon's hunt while he headed off to meet Ike for lunch.

CHAPTER 5

Tuck and Ike Baumgarner decided to pick up a flounder sandwich at the Ocean Fish Market, and then walk down the along the river where there was less chance to be overheard.

"Ike, I need for you to get a bag of drink glasses to Detectives Banks and Loveless in Columbia and see if they can quietly find some prints on them that could tell us who we are dealing with. When do you think that you can make that run?" Tuck asked around the side of his sandwich, taking every precaution not to be eavesdropped on.

"Well, I just happen to have a fellow that has to be up there this evening about the time those two come on duty if I remember correctly. We could probably have an answer tomorrow. Well, that could hinge on whether you sprung for some really fresh donuts or not!" Ike had a big grin on his face just thinking how stereotypical those two detectives were when it came to donuts. In stark contrast to Tuck and himself, both of those men were fairly rotund from sitting too much and eating sweets at every opportunity.

"Done!" Tuck replied, "Let's walk back to the truck and I'll get those glasses for you. Here's a twenty for some donuts when your man gets up there. We certainly want them fresh!"

The radio was going nuts when they reached the truck, "Lieutenant Tucker, come in. Lieutenant Tucker, come in please." Tuck grabbed the mike and responded, "This is Lieutenant Tucker, over."

"Lieutenant, this is Biggs. I just shot a big red wolf coming out of that trail, over"

"Private, I thought we were shooting the cougar tonight. It is just barely afternoon," Tuck sounded a little put out with Biggs, although he knew that the man had good judgment. The next words were incredible.

"I wasn't going to shoot, sir, but that wolf had an arm in his mouth!" Replied Private Biggs

"WHAT! What did you say, an 'arm'?" Tuck was so shocked that he was almost tongue-tied. Ike was just standing there with his mouth open. Both men were having a hard time believing what they were hearing.

"Yes sir, it is an arm. The thing is chewed up pretty bad, but there is a hand on the end with a wedding band. What do you want me to do?"

"Just stand by. I am on the way. Deputy Baumgarner will handle forensics and get everyone rolling to your location, and Biggs, nice work!" Tucker out.

Tuck handed Ike the bag, then said, "I'm rolling to his location Ike. We were just off Punch Bowl Road on the power line to the right. See you up there."

"Right behind you Tuck, my boy, and to think that I said it was going to be a boring day!" Ike replied as he leaned into his car to make the calls.

Tuck was rolling back down highway 701 toward Cates Bay Road at seventy miles an hour when he looked in the rearview mirror and saw the WLIB News van, and the red-haired reporter, Maggie O'Brien, pulling close to him.

"This is all that I need right now," Tuck thought, "another animal killing on the eleven o'clock news! The Colonel is going to be pissed!"

With that, he turned on his lights and siren while his foot found the floorboard under the gas pedal. When he made the turn onto Cates Bay Road, the van had dropped back about a half mile. Tuck kept the speed down through the residential area then turned it up when the road opened up.

"Private Biggs, come in," Tuck keyed the mike and called Biggs.

"Biggs here, sir," Was the reply

"News crews behind me, Private, look sharp, Tucker out," He should call the Colonel, but the phone reception was bad out here, and he really needed two hands while running the big truck at close to ninety miles an hour.

When Tuck reached the turn off for the right of way, Biggs had already pulled his truck down to the area where he had shot the wolf...if it was a wolf. Tuck was having a tough time digesting that bit of news. Of course, hunters had said for years that some of the animals that had been seen out here were too big for coyotes, but the DNR gave the reports little credence. There was some speculation that the red wolf was a cross between the coyote and the western gray wolf, which would mean that it was an import, and there was the viewpoint that said the red wolf was its own distinct species. There was no official view that held the red wolf to be in the South Carolina swampland, so Tuck was anxious to see what Biggs had shot.

The big-bodied wolf was lying on its side about twenty feet in the front of the truck. A couple of feet closer to the truck lay what looked to be the arm that Biggs had called about.

"How about that shot, sir?" Biggs asked with a big smile on his face. The bullet had struck the animal in the left shoulder and exited the other side leaving a gaping wound.

"Nice shooting, Private. That is all of five hundred yards with a borrowed rifle...very nice shooting indeed," Tuck was impressed. There was probably a great deal about Private Biggs that he didn't know, but he certainly wasn't making an empty boast about his shooting prowess.

Biggs directed his attention to the arm that was drawing flies. They both knelt down to examine it closer when Tuck noticed that it seemed to belong to an old man. "Look at these spots where the skin isn't torn, private. Doesn't this look like an old person's skin to you?"

"Yes sir, it does. He would have been a pretty good sized man too, if what is left of the muscle is any indication," Biggs answered.

Tuck went to the truck and dragged out a map of the area. Using the game trail entrance and exits from the power line as a reference, he drew a line intersecting Old Pee Dee Highway, then called Deputy Baumgarner to see if he would send a couple of deputies to check houses in the area.

"Well, Tuck, the only old fellow that I know in the general area that you are describing would be Cyrus Bean, but he is a good bit off the highway down toward the swamp. I'll check that out myself and get back to you. The coroner and the forensics team are on the way, and that red-headed reporter is almost on you. Over and out," Ike signed off with what seemed to be a chuckle over the last part of the transmission since he knew how short Tuck's patience was with reporters.

"Private, get a tarp out of my truck and cover that arm up before the reporters get here, will you please?" Tuck asked in a respectful tone while he took one last look at the arm then moved his attention to the wolf. He certainly had not seen anything like this before. The animal was close to ninety pounds and looked like a very large coyote, except that the head was much shorter. "Great, that's all we need, bigger coyotes in the swamp," Tuck said to no one in particular as he stood up from the dead wolf. For the present, he would say that it was a 'coy-dog' part dog and part coyote. It wouldn't sit so well with Colonel McNeery to have another species of man-killer in the swamp being reported on the news tonight.

"Lieutenant Tucker, Lieutenant Tucker!" with a waving arm, Maggie O'Brien jumped out of the WLIB News van and started toward Tuck.

With a groan, Tuck walked toward Maggie to greet her and to keep her away from the scene until the coroner's men had a look.

"Hello, Maggie. I can't let you go any closer to the coy-dog until we get the medics out of here. You understand, don't you?"

"That's all right Lieutenant Tucker," Maggie said in a professional tone holding the microphone to her mouth. The cameraman was right behind her and the camera was rolling, "What can you tell us about the arm? Who does it belong to?"

Tuck tried to be as evasive as he could, but the radio transmission had been heard by Maggie and her cameraman so they knew about the arm, "No Maggie, we don't have any information yet, but as soon as we know anything, I will let you know."

Several sheriffs' deputies arrived and started taping off the area while the forensics team took pictures. It gave Tuck a chance to move away from the news crew while their attention was diverted. He heard the radio in his truck, "Come in Lieutenant Tucker, over," It was Ike.

"Go ahead for Lieutenant Tucker," Tuck answered.

"You need to get over here to the Bean residence; I found what is left of Cyrus," Ike stated flatly, "Pass that on to the coroner also if you will Tuck. It looks like Earl's killer got Cyrus also."

Tuck went over to Joel Biggs and quietly told him what was going on, "Keep everything quiet over here, Joel. I will go over to the Bean's place. Wait until I back out to tell the coroner,"

"Yes, sir. I'll handle it," Biggs replied, "Oh uh, Lieutenant, I've still got your rifle in the truck. Do you want me to get it for you?"

"Just clean it for me, and I'll get it in the morning. And Joel, you did a good job," Tuck answered with a smile as he walked briskly to his truck.

The heavy Ford was sideways on the sand of Punch Bowl Road as Tuck ran it right on the edge of control in his haste to get to Cyrus Bean's cabin. Ike must have seen something to make him think that the cougar had killed Cyrus, but what? The wolf carrying the arm had Tuck stumped also. Why would it be running into an open area with a body part in its mouth like a jackal, unless something was chasing it? In the ten minutes that it took for Tuck to arrive at the spot that Ike was waiting, a dozen different scenarios ran through his mind.

Ike was standing in the front of the small bluegrass special that Cyrus Bean had called home for so many years. The twelve hundred square foot house had screened porches front and back but still seemed too small for anyone to have raised a family in.

"Hey Tuck, it's around back," Ike spoke softly, "I'm glad I didn't eat anything heavy today. This is a real mess."

As they walked around the house and into the backyard, Tuck thought about how Cyrus and his wife must have been happy here. Somehow, it seemed natural that the spot that Ike indicated, as the place where Cyrus' remains lay was also the final resting place of his late wife.

The ground over the grave was covered in blood, torn flesh, and what was left of Cyrus' overalls. The ground was also covered in coyote tracks that obliterated the one track that Tuck wanted to see.

"Look over here, Tuck," Ike called. He was standing in a clump of taller grass that obscured Tuck's view. When he stepped over for a closer look, the head of Cyrus Bean was lying face down. In the back of the skull that had been stripped of most of its flesh were the signature puncture wounds of a big cougar.

"I'd better call the Colonel," Tuck said as he pulled his cell phone out, then in a frustrated tone said, "Great…just great! Now there is no signal! I'm going back to the truck and use the radio. Just pray that Maggie O'Brien isn't near her truck."

"I've got to make some calls also," Ike replied as he followed Tuck back to the front of the house.

Tuck decided against the radio so he would have to drive to a location where he could get a signal. The coroner was on the way, and all of the animals involved had to be miles away by now.

"I'll be back after I talk to the Colonel, Ike. It will start a panic if Maggie and the WLIB crew break another cougar attack on the six o'clock news. Try to keep it about coyotes finding a body as long as possible."

"I'll hold down the fort here, Tuck. Find out if we are going to hunt this thing so I can call in some of our volunteers," Ike responded.

Tuck gave him a wave, drove out to the Old Pee Dee Highway, and then took a left that would bring him into the range of a cell tower by the time he reached the Hunting Swamp Bridge.

CHAPTER 6

The coyotes had found her kill just as the one hundred and eighty pound female was getting ready to bury Cyrus' remains under some leaves and dirt at the edge of the yard. Rushing in from several directions, they distracted her enough for the pack leader to start ripping and tearing at the body while the others worried the big cat. Finally, she ran off into the night with a snarl to wait for the coyotes to finish and leave. She would return to her kill after a much-needed sleep. The trauma of losing her kittens was still fresh on her mind and coupled with the long night had taken a toll on her physically. She found a live oak about a half of a mile from the Bean residence and climbed to an overhanging limb to sleep undisturbed.

It was late morning when the cougar jumped gracefully from her perch in the big oak tree. After testing the wind for smells and sounds of danger, she headed back to her kill to see if anything was left. She needed a few more pounds of meat to keep her strength and size with the kitten still nursing, and she didn't feel like another stalk this morning.

The big wolf was tearing at what was left of Cyrus' arm when the cat came to the edge of the yard. As she loosed a guttural snarl of rage and warning, the wolf pulled the arm loose and leaped for the wood line opposite the cougar. She made two jumps in his direction and then turned back to inspect the kill. Finding nothing left, she ran after the wolf in a rage, intent on taking the last morsel of meat away from him, even if it meant a fight to the death. Besides, he was just a big dog, and she had developed a taste for dogs.

She was within ten feet of the wolf as he burst into the semi-clearing of the right-of-way; when suddenly, and with a loud smacking sound, he was spun violently to the right, and his body turned a complete flip. In a matter of a split second, before the spray of blood and hair could settle, the loud boom of the .308 Winchester signaled just what had happened to the wolf, and the cat instinctively spun around and ran at top speed away from the area. She ran parallel to the right-of-way for almost a mile before finding a small ditch that she could crawl in without being spotted. Moving carefully, the cougar made the return trip to her kitten so that he could nurse before she hunted again.

CHAPTER 7

"Lieutenant Tucker!" barked the voice on the other end of the phone call, "I am getting vague reports that there is something going on down there. What have you got?"

"Well, Colonel, we had had another killing last night. I am almost certain that it was a cougar attack, but Private Biggs shot a red wolf that was running with an arm in its mouth just a few hundred yards from the attack site, so the media believes that it is a coyote attack. I would like to keep it that way for as long as we can if that suits you," Tuck replied.

"Absolutely lieutenant, let's sit on this as long as possible. What makes you think that this is a cougar attack?" Colonel McNeery sounded tired.

"As you know, Colonel, we found the shoe last night that matches what Earl Johnson had on when he disappeared, then Deputy Baumgarner found Cyrus Bean's head when we back-tracked the wolf to the kill site. It has the evidence of a big cat bite at the base of the skull. It looks like the coyotes might have run the cougar off the kill," Tuck continued, "Do I have permission to thin these coyotes out? They've tasted human flesh and probably have lost their fear of man over it. I certainly wouldn't want them to grab a child."

"Get a hunt up. I am going to relax restrictions on the taking of these animals, but only you or Private Biggs will be allowed measures other than shooting or trapping. We will allow night hunting with centerfire rifles and lights until you can bring that coyote population under control. I don't want any surprises on the eleven o'clock news, so keep this as quiet as you can," Colonel McNeery hung up.

Tuck turned the truck around and headed back to the Bean residence. Recent history had taught him whom he should contact for more innovative ways to kill these coyotes. The cat would be a different story.

As he pulled into the long drive that led to Cyrus' house, all that he could think about was the circus that awaited him at the other end of the long stream of vehicles that almost blocked the narrow drive. In addition to the medical examiner's van, the film crew from WLIB was there, along with two more sheriff deputies and several civilians. It started as soon as he got out of the truck.

"Lieutenant Tucker, can we get a statement?" was the first shout that he heard coming from Maggie O'Brien who was already filming his arrival.

"Hello, Maggie," Tuck responded, "It looks like Mr. Bean might have been attacked by a pack of coyotes last night. We can't give you definite proof until the medical examiner finishes his report, but the coy-dog that Private Biggs shot had Mr. Bean's arm in his mouth which kind of points to a coyote attack being responsible."

"I can tell you that we are going to do everything possible to reduce this pack's numbers within the next couple of days, so there is nothing for your viewers to fear if they just keep their kids close, and make certain that the family dog is tied up. Now I have to get back to the scene," Tuck finished.

"Thank you, Lieutenant," He heard as Maggie finished her broadcast. He walked through the crowd of onlookers that were gawking at the area where the medical examiner and his men were working to recover as much of Cyrus Bean's remains as possible. "Hey Ike!" he shouted as he got closer to the deputy, "I need to talk to you a minute over here," and Tuck gestured with his hand to a spot away from the crowd of neighbors.

Ike walked over shaking his head at the large number of spectators that had gathered, "News sure travels fast," then, "What's going on, Tuck? Did the Colonel have a stroke when you told him?"

"He had already heard some of the news. When I told him about the cougar, he was almost relaxed about it, well, as relaxed as he gets anyway," Both men shared a brief chuckle over that and then got down to business.

"Ike, I need a report on those glasses as soon as possible. It looks like we will be tied up down here hunting for at least a week, but I would like to know who is watching us so I can figure out how to cover my back end if you know what I mean," Tuck spoke bluntly.

"I'll get them to Columbia tonight with some kind of story involved. Your name won't be mentioned. Do you need me to help with this hunt? Are we going after a cougar?" Ike asked.

"Nope, we are going to kill off a few of these coyotes first. I don't even want a mention of a cougar attack until McNeery okays issuing that information. If you know of some fellows that would like to night-hunt these coyotes for me, have them get in touch with the office so we can set it up. All things are on the table now and that includes night hunting, electronic calls, centerfire rifles, and big lights," Tuck replied.

"Well, you know that the weather is going to take a turn late this evening. We are supposed to get a drop in temperature and a good bit of rain for the next couple of days anyway. What kind of time frame are you looking at for the hunt?" Ike asked as he started back to his car.

"I'm starting tomorrow," Was Tuck's quick reply, "We can plan the main body of the men to be in the woods when it clears up, but anyone that wants to hunt with me is welcome to come along. Oh, and Ike, keep me posted on the lab results for those glasses, Okay?"

"Sure thing Tuck. I'll see you tomorrow," Ike said as they parted company. Then, over his shoulder, "Hey, you be careful!"

Tuck just smiled and waved to his friend as he walked to his truck. There was a lot to do if they were going to be successful in thinning the coyotes out. Those animals adapted to men's hunting techniques very quickly, and Tuck knew that they would have to hit them with several methods of extermination at one time if they wanted even a slim chance of success. He decided to let Joel Biggs deal with the medical examiner and the sheriff's department to finish up at the Bean residence, so Tuck could head back to the office to get started on planning his hunt. His first call was to Hanna to let her know that he would be late, not that she was surprised at this bit of news, and then a quick call to Harry Albright to fill him in on the latest developments.

"Listen, Son, Bob and I were listening to the latest news reports and both of us are itching to help with your hunt. Do you think that you could put up with two old codgers for a couple of days?" Harry asked jokingly.

In the background, Tuck heard, "Codger, speak for yourself! I've only been retired for a couple of months!" as Bob joined the conversation.

"You know, I could use some help on this, and my new fellows don't have the experience that you two have, how about both of you meeting me at the house in the morning and we will discuss it over breakfast," Tuck was tickled that his old partner would be there to help him, unofficially of course, but it was still good to have Bob Pike back in the area.

CHAPTER 8

"Hey Teddy, we've got what looks like a homicide out on one of those old horse farms on 378," Detective Alvarez Banks called across the desk to his partner, Detective Teddy Loveless in the Columbia, South Carolina police station's homicide division where they had been stuck on the graveyard shift for the past several months. Teddy seemed to think that it was some form of retribution for uncovering the evidence against the late Lawrence Richards, Under Secretary of the Department of the Interior, U.S. Fish and Wildlife Service that had threatened to embroil the entire government in a conspiracy scandal. The much-reported cougar attacks and killings in the Myrtle Beach area and the attempted murders of the two DNR enforcement officers and their families had brought the matter into the national spotlight but little was achieved except to force the guilty parties that had survived to go underground.

"Have they got an I.D. on the body?" Teddy asked as he slipped on his well-worn tweed jacket over a sweater vest. The February warm spell was over, and the cool night air reminded his joints why they wanted him to retire in Florida.

"Nope; it looks like the stiff was buried in horse manure for a while. Kind of like us," Al finished with a chuckle, "Let's grab some coffee, and get out there for a look."

The old farm had once been a showplace with its beautifully kept pastures, white board fences, long drive, and pristine stables. Now it had been deserted since the economy had crashed in 2009, and most of the fencing had rotted away, the pastures were overgrown with weeds, and the barns sat vacant and silent. Al and Teddy drove down the quarter of a mile long driveway to the first barn where the flashing lights of the police cars and the coroner's wagon showed them the location of the corpse.

"We didn't want to move anything until you boys got out here," Jeff, the night assistant to the medical examiner greeted them sleepily, "Some teenagers snuck their car in here to park. The boy got out to take a leak and saw a foot sticking out of the pile of horse crap. You wanna take a statement from them first so they can get home?"

"I'll get their statement, Al. You check out the stiff," Teddy volunteered. He always felt like it was his job to give Al as much support as possible to ease the load that he seemed to carry since the death of his wife.

Jeff and his helper had cleaned the horse manure from the top of the corpse as carefully as possible, but the state of decomposition made the task difficult. The body lay face down with its arms bound behind the back with what looked like twine, and the bare skull on the back of the head showed five small holes that were midway up the head from the base of the skull.

"This looks like a hit," Al said to Jeff, "How long do you think that it has been in here?"

"Well, the old manure might accelerate decomposition, but I would guess probably about three months. We'll know more tomorrow after the boss does an autopsy."

"I'm going to help Teddy with those statements; can you have all of that delivered to my desk by tomorrow evening?" Al asked.

"I'll send what we have Al, if there is anything odd, I'll call you personally," Jeff replied.

"If you can get that identity to me as soon as possible, I will buy you a cup of coffee when you come over," Al offered the cup of what had been described as the 'worst coffee on the planet' with a laugh.

Teddy Loveless was just finishing with the witnesses when Al came over, "Need any help here, Teddy?" he asked.

"No, we are just finishing up. Did you see anything interesting over there?" Teddy answered.

"It will be tomorrow before we get a chance at this one, although I believe it was a hit of some sort. The head had five small caliber holes in the back of the skull, and the hands were tied behind its back," Al replied, "Let's head back in and start the paperwork. Maybe someone put a fresh pot of coffee on."

"How about we hit that Waffle House up on John Byrne Parkway before we head back instead? I've got a taste for eggs and hash browns. Besides, the coffee has to be better than that stuff at the station," Teddy retorted.

"As long as I can get some Rolaids, I'm in for the coffee," Al threw back as they headed for the car. There was something bothering him about this killing that a good cup of coffee and something sweet might help settle.

CHAPTER 9

"Michael Tucker, it is after midnight! Will you please come to bed?" Hanna's sleepy voice called out from the bedroom.

Tuck was sitting at his desk in the same den that the late Lawrence Richards had threatened Bob Pike in just a few short months ago. All of that seemed like yesterday to Tuck, and the events of the past couple of days just seemed to bring those memories closer to the surface. Sitting here in the quiet room helped him to think, and he still needed to come up with a plan for the morning's hunt.

"I'm coming, Love," Tuck responded.

Hanna was his first concern. The pregnancy was routine, which had to be a miracle. She was healing nicely from the broken bones and muscle tears that resulted from the attempt on her life, but the doctors were more concerned about the long-term effects of the brain trauma that the impact had caused. Even they viewed the recovery as somewhat miraculous, but only in hushed tones when the family wasn't present. Harry Albright, Hanna's father, was more outspoken about her healing. As far as he was concerned, God had delivered his little girl in answer to the fervent prayers that were given for her. Tuck was inclined to agree, but couldn't really vocalize why he did.

"Did you let Weston out for a bit, Hon?" Hanna asked when he slid into bed. She didn't want the one hundred and thirty-pound yellow lab to wake them any earlier than he had to.

"I did earlier. He is sleeping by the hall door, and I didn't want to bother him again," Tuck replied as he kissed the back of Hanna's neck and gave her a hug as he snuggled against her for a short night of sleep. The day had been very long, and he drifted off almost immediately.

Hanna lay awake for another thirty minutes or so, her mind busy thinking about all that was going on in her life. As if the baby arriving in just a few short months wasn't enough to think about, she now had concerns about the people that had followed them, the animal attacks, and having to meet Maggie O'Brien for lunch tomorrow. She was still acting out different scenarios in her mind when she drifted into a fitful sleep.

Tuck woke with a start to the sound of Weston growling at someone knocking at the back door. One glance at the clock told him that he had forgotten to set the alarm, and it was already after six o' clock.

"Weston, shut up you dumb dog, it's only Harry and Bob," He shouted after looking out the bedroom window. Tuck made his way to the door and let his father-in-law and Bob Pike into the kitchen.

"Good Morning Tuck," Bob greeted him in a cheerful tone, "I thought we were going to get an early start; hope we didn't wake you."

"Good morning son," Harry said while giving Tuck a brief fatherly hug.

"I forgot to set the alarm last night. The coffee is already brewed, but it might be a little old now," Tuck told them as he poured three cups of black coffee.

Harry Albright thanked Tuck as he took the cup that was offered him, "I'll need some milk in this Tuck. It looks a little strong."

Bob took the cup and thanked him saying, "Just the way that I like it, Tuck. So, what exactly are we going to do today?"

"Bob, do you remember that poacher that we busted with the conibear traps last year?" Tuck asked. Before he could get a reply, Hanna appeared in the doorway looking bright and very pregnant.

"Hi Daddy, Tuck didn't tell me that you were coming up," then, "Hold it you two. I am going to fix us all breakfast so let's get the orders in before there is anymore shop talking," She gave her dad and Bob a big hug, and Tuck a kiss before getting the eggs and bacon out of the refrigerator, "If we are going hunting, we need to keep our strength up."

"We…? You are not going with us. The weather has turned cold and wet, and you don't need to be in it. Besides, we are setting traps for coyotes, and Weston would find a way to get hurt," Tuck replied forcefully.

Hanna just gave him a grin and said, "I was just joking Mr. Tucker. Now, how many eggs do you men want?"

After putting in his order for bacon, eggs, and grits, Bob Pike responded to Tuck's question about the traps, "I remember that guy, Tuck. He killed a couple of his neighbor's dogs by accident with those sets of his. Pretty darned efficient, even if they were illegal. Why do you ask?"

"Well, I was thinking of setting those conibears for these coyotes along with some other things that are highly illegal and probably immoral, if you get my meaning. Do you remember where they are stored?" Tuck replied

"Since you don't know, then it is obvious that you haven't cleaned out the old storage barn out back. They were in an old pasteboard barrel in the corner out there," Bob said with a chuckle, "I didn't keep the buckets, though."

After breakfast, Tuck, Harry, and Bob went into the back yard to the storage barn that Bob had built on the property. Sure enough, buried beneath a layer of junk that Tuck had been meaning to go through, was the dilapidated barrel with twenty, rusty conibear traps inside.

"We'll have to boil these in some walnut husks if they are going to be of any use," Bob observed, "Is that old gas fish cooker still around?"

"I haven't gotten around to going through anything that you left, Bob. Things have been pretty hectic. I think that old cast iron wash kettle is still here also. I'll go over to the fence and pick up some walnuts to throw in," Tuck said as he reached for an old bucket that was sitting in the barn. The walnut tree on the neighbor's property caused a mess in the fall when the fruit dropped off, but Tuck was certainly glad that it was here now, as the rotten husks would give plenty of scent cover for the traps.

"I'll drag out the kettle and get everything set up," Harry replied. Soon the men had a steaming wash kettle of boiling water with walnut husks set up on the gas fired fish cooker.

"Bob, Harry, if you all can keep an eye on these for me, I can get to the office and set everything else up," Tuck asked.

"Whatever you need Tuck," Harry said with a smile. He thought of Tuck as his son, and it seemed as if he had always been part of the family.

"It will probably take an hour to boil the rust smell out of these. I'll give you a call when they are ready," was Bob's response, "It is kind of exciting to be going back out again Tuck. I appreciate you letting me in on this."

"I can't think of anyone that I would rather have with me, Bob," Tuck said as he walked to the truck.

It seemed natural for Bob to be involved, even though he was no longer a part of the DNR. They had been through more together than most men had, and Tuck was concerned that there were too many loose ends unraveling that could be a snare to all of them. With Bob's help, he hoped to be able to tie a few of them up.

"I'm going to pick up a few five-gallon pails also while I am out. Is there anything else that we need?"

"Just the bait but a few old chickens will work for that," Bob replied knowing that Tuck knew where to find them.

The weather was certainly nasty for setting traps and the forecast did not call for any improvement for the next two days, so Tuck decided to spend the time arranging for the coyote hunt that he hoped would take the dominant dog out of commission. It was well known that the pack would probably break up if the lead coyote were killed, so they had to take every precaution to make sure that happened.

Tuck called Joel Biggs on his radio, "Private Biggs, what is your location? Is Private Knowles with you this morning?" He asked.

"Good morning Lieutenant!" came the reply, "I do have Private Knowles with me and we are heading into the office. I've also got your rifle cleaned up. Is there any chance that you want to sell it? She is a beauty."

Tuck knew that Biggs was joking about buying the rifle, but he responded with a laugh in the negative anyway. He had built the customized Remington 700, its fluted 24" E.R. Shaw barrel chambered for the .308 Winchester and topped with a Leupold Mark 4 M5 when he had first joined the DNR after coming back from Afghanistan. It was a piece of precision equipment as Joel Biggs had demonstrated when he made the five hundred yard shot on the running red wolf the day before.

"I'll meet you at the office, Private. There won't be any patrols today so you both can help with getting this hunt organized," Tuck finished up on the radio and then made a call to Ike on his cell phone.

"Good morning, Ike. Are you coming in this morning?" Tuck asked when Ike answered the phone.

"Only if you are buying coffee, my friend," Ike responded good-naturedly, "I've got some news for you when I get there."

Ike met Tuck at the Hardee's restaurant and gave him the briefing on what was found on the glasses that Tuck had sent to be analyzed.

"It didn't take long to identify one of the prints, Tuck. They belong to an escort named Courtney Wells that works the beach area when she is not teaching school upstate. Two sets of prints belong to RIOZ employees and one that is not in any database. DNA results won't be back for a few days, but I wouldn't expect any surprises. Either the guy is nobody, or he is very professional about keeping his identity concealed," Ike told him, "I think that you need to be very careful."

"Boy, I sure was hoping that this had all gone away, but with the government being involved, that might have been too much to hope for," Tuck responded, "Can you send someone over to talk to Miss Wells and see if she will identify her 'friend' for us?"

"I called it into one of our detectives in Myrtle Beach already. Hopefully, we will know something within the hour," was Ike's response as he headed for his patrol car, "Thanks for the breakfast, Tuck. I'll call as soon as there is word."

CHAPTER 10

The cold rain that drenched the swamp forced the cougar to find shelter for her kitten and herself, and the only thing that offered any relief was an old fallen cypress that had rotted out on the inside, leaving a hollow just long enough for her to get them both out of the weather. She would nurse the kitten this evening, but her hunger was driving her desire to hunt, and game would be scarce until the storm passed. At least the storm would force the coyotes into their dens so that she could feel somewhat safe in their cramped quarters, still she only slept fitfully during the early morning, waking at every noise.

The big alpha male leader of the coyote pack that had been taking so many of the cougar's kills lay at the entrance to his den listening to the sounds of the stormy night and sampling the gusts of cold air that swirled past him as his mate for life slept curled behind him. At sixty-five pounds, he was the largest dog in the pack and the most aggressive when it came time to kill. This was due primarily to his father being a full-blooded red wolf and his mother a beta coyote female from the last generation of the pack. Although the odds of him surviving past the first few weeks of his life were very low, largely because the previous alpha male would naturally only feed his own offspring that were produced with the alpha female, the young coy/wolf managed to survive on scraps until he was able to forage for himself. The lack of extremely cold weather in the low country of South Carolina meant an abundance of small game year round, but the pack rule that the alpha male ate first of any kill resulted in the young hybrid being chased out of the pack. He had eaten a fat rabbit before the alpha male of the pack and the alpha female fed.

For almost a year the coy/wolf avoided the areas frequented by the pack, preferring to stay close to human habitations where the occasional meal of stray cat or opossums that raided the local trashcans coupled with the geese that thrived in almost every pond kept him healthy and growing to his full body weight. Only then did his strong wolf instinct lead him back into the range of the coyote pack where his presence was soon discovered.

Once the scent of the coy/wolf was in the nostrils of the pack leader the rest of the dogs took up the chase to find the interloper, only to find that he had been hunting them. Taking them by surprise the big coy/wolf, weighing twenty pounds more than his rival, attacked the older alpha male with a characteristic wolf-like ferocity. The fight was short lived as his more powerful jaws clamped on the throat of his adversary and tore into the muscle and arteries of the neck. As the old alpha male lay dying, the rest of the pack submitted to this new leader that would soon lead them on a reign of terror in the swamp and adjoining forests. That first winter, he took a mate from among the pack, a strong young female that showed all of the traits of an alpha female, and she birthed a litter of twelve pups that first spring, six of whom survived infancy. By the fourth year of his leadership, his offspring numbered thirty-two, twelve of whom were in his pack, which had grown from six coyotes to twenty-three. He had turned the pack into a very efficient hunting and killing machine, due largely to the increased size and aggressiveness of the coy/wolf offspring, and they had become a real threat to the deer, turkey, and feral hog populations in the river bottoms. Tonight, however, the pack rested comfortably in their dens, waiting for the easing of the rain before the leader signaled another hunt.

Before daybreak, the rain subsided, and the cougar, driven by hunger, slipped out of her temporary shelter after whistling a warning to her kitten to stay put until she returned. She would hunt this morning along one of the many game trails that ran through the river bottom. Shortly after first light, a young whitetail buck made his way along the trail that the cat was watching and walked unsuspectingly within a few feet of the cougar. She was on him in an instant, burying her teeth into the neck and sinking her needle-like claws into his shoulders as she wrestled him to the ground. The deer fought for his life by kicking and struggling, but to no avail. Once the cougar fastened onto his throat, death came quickly, and the cat dragged the carcass off the trail and into the thick scrub where she could feed unmolested. The kitten would nurse when she returned, and then they would hunt for a new den away from the territory that the pack of coyotes had claimed. When she had eaten her fill from the ninety-pound deer, she covered the remains, even though it was unlikely that she would return to this kill.

CHAPTER 11

It was raining when Tuck pulled back into the driveway with the supplies for the hunt just as Bob and Harry were finishing up their preparations inside of the small storage barn.

"Whew, what is that nasty smell?" Tuck asked as he came into the barn with a supply of buckets.

"Harry just whipped up a 'sure fire' concoction to take care of the coyotes," Bob said laughingly.

Harry took the top off one of his two buckets to show Tuck.

"This is probably illegal in all fifty states, but it will certainly get rid of the most stupid members of the pack!" he exclaimed.

Tuck held his breath to take a look inside of the bucket and saw a mixture of old ground meat and something bluish-gray in color that looked like bits of sponge.

"What in the world is that stuff?" he asked Harry.

"A mixture of old hamburger meat and some rat poison that I picked up at the builder supply. We just form it into softball sized balls and leave it along their trail," He replied, "It will do the same thing to the coyotes that it does to rats, and it won't be pretty."

"Bob, do you remember how those buckets were fitted for the traps? I've got five here that we can rig," Tuck said as he put the buckets down.

"Yep, you just slot the sides of the bucket so that the springs on the trap will slide down and leave the trap about six inches inside of the bucket top. The top gets a hole about nine inches round so the coyote can get his head in, and, presto, dead coyote," Bob replied, "I'll get them fitted right away."

Harry, what are you doing with those turtle hooks?" Tuck asked his father-in-law.

"Well this may sound a bit gruesome, but we are going to rig these with about six feet of marlin wire and hang them from tree limbs a couple of feet off the ground with a piece of chicken hooked on for bait. The coyote jumps up to take the chicken and gets hooked up like a big fish," Harry replied.

Tuck turned toward the house, shaking his head, "You two are something else. I'm going in to see Hanna for a few minutes. Oh, if anyone comes over, please hide that stuff. I'd hate for it to get out that DNR officers were engaging in acts of animal cruelty."

Harry and Bob just laughed at the suggestion and got back to work. Both were eager to get the traps and bait out into the swamp where it would be put to good use.

As Tuck opened the door of the house, he heard Hanna call to him, "Tuck, come quick, and look at this!"

"Look at what, Love? I'm kind of busy right now!" He responded.

"It's about some poor girl being murdered. I think that we've seen her before...somewhere!" Hanna called out, "Hurry!"

Tuck entered the living room in time to see the face of the girl that had been in RIOZ the night before. It was the face of Courtney Wells, and she had been murdered!

"I've got to get hold of Ike, Hanna, this is important!" Tuck said in a hurried tone as he pulled his cell phone out of his pocket and speed-dialed Ike's number.

"Hey Tuck, what's going on?" Ike answered.

"Ike, that escort was murdered last night!" Tuck exclaimed, "Can you get us all of the information on the killing?

"I'm in Myrtle Beach right now, Tuck. I'll get over to the crime scene and see what I can find out. Should I let on about the fingerprints to the locals?" Ike replied.

"I know that it would probably be the right thing to do, but let's sit on the information until the Myrtle Beach boys gather all of their evidence," Tuck responded.

"Will do! I'll call this afternoon if anything interesting turns up down there," Ike finished the call.

Hanna was standing in the doorway to the living room looking at Tuck when the call ended. "You mean that was the girl that was spying on us last night? That's horrible, Tuck!" Who was the guy that she was with?"

"We don't know yet, Hon. He doesn't have any fingerprints on record. I'm going back outside to let Harry and Bob know. Don't worry about any of this. We'll handle anything that comes up, I promise," Tuck said as he gave her a big hug and then went out of the house.

Bob saw the look in Tuck's eyes as he walked in the light rain back to the shed, "Hey Tuck, what's going on?"

"Do you guys remember the couple that sat over to my right hand about three tables over at RIOZ last night; the ones that we got the glasses from?" Tuck asked, "I had those glasses checked for prints, just in case, and one set of the prints belongs to a girl that was found dead a few minutes ago in Myrtle Beach!"

"Good Lord!" Harry exclaimed, "It looks like this stuff is starting back up again. We need to be very careful from now on."

"Tuck, did you get a good look at the man that she was with?" Bob asked.

"You know, Bob, it is funny. I saw the man's face, but nothing sticks in my mind about him. He could be anyone," Tuck responded in a worried tone.

"Well, he is a professional, I'm certain of it. Why else would the girl be dead except to keep his identity a secret? Have you got a piece that I can put in my pocket for a little insurance, Tuck? I had to sell all of my firearms before we went to Honduras," Bob asked.

"Bob, I've got just the thing," Harry replied before Tuck could answer, "I've got a little 'J' frame Smith and Wesson Air Weight in .38 Special with the hammer bobbed that will get the job done. You are welcome to it!"

"Well guys, the rain is letting up, let's go make a few bucket sets, and maybe some dry land fishing as well. Those coyotes are just another problem in a growing list that we have to take care of. We may as well get started. I'll keep you all posted as soon as Ike calls me," Tuck said as he picked up four buckets and started for the truck.

Bob and Harry got the rest of the gear loaded while Tuck told Hanna where he was going. Soon they were headed to the swamp close to the scene of the latest attacks. With any luck, the pack would be much smaller in the morning!

CHAPTER 12

Ike arrived at the run-down motel where Courtney Wells' body had been found and found Homicide Detective Steve Rogers standing by his car talking to the red-hair reporter, Maggie O'Brian, "Maggie, that's all I know, I swear!"

"Okay Steve, but you will keep me informed if there are any new developments, won't you?" Maggie gave him a big smile that seemed to hold a promise.

"You bet Maggie! You'll be the first person I call if anything breaks," Detective Rogers said as she walked away, "Oh, Hey Ike. What brings you by?"

"Hi Steve, I heard the report on this and was curious. What have you got?" Ike responded.

"Well, we don't want this in the news, but that girl didn't O.D. like I told Maggie. She had three small caliber bullet wounds in the back of her head!" The detective replied.

"Murdered...do you have a suspect yet?" Ike pushed for a little more information.

"No, although a fellow dropped her off last night. The strange thing is that nobody could give us a description of him that wouldn't fit ninety percent of everyone at the beach! We might turn up something with the ballistics when they come back. People that kill like this have generally done it before. Maybe he used the same gun somewhere else," Detective Rogers finished.

"Here's hoping Steve. I've got to run," Ike said as he walked back to his car. His hand was on the cell phone even as he pulled away from the sleazy motel. Tuck needed to know about this immediately!

Tuck's cell phone vibrated in his pocket while he was ankle deep in the black mud down in the swamp bottom. The rain from the evening and this morning had revived the mosquitoes also which swarmed around the exposed parts of the men's faces and hands.

"Hey Ike, what's going on?" Tuck answered.

Harry and Bob scouted ahead for visible signs or trails that might be used by the pack when it was hunting.

"Tuck, the girl was murdered; shot three times in the back of the head with a small caliber round. I thought that you should know," Ike reported.

"Thanks, Ike. I'm in a bad place for phone receptions and you are breaking up pretty bad. I'll call when we come out," Tuck responded then to Harry and Bob, "Hey Guys, we've got some news!"

"Yeah Tuck. What is it?" Harry replied as he and Bob walked back to where Tuck stood in the mud.

"That girl was murdered! Ike just told me that she was shot three times in the back of the head with something small. It looks like we are going to have to start living a paranoid life again," Tuck told them.

"Well, let's finish up these sets and get back to town. This is going to call for some masterly strategizing if we are going to stay on top of the situation," Bob replied.

"I agree," Harry said, "I'm going to try and find Anthony Morris if I can. It seemed to me that he was on our side of this mess."

"That is a good idea, Dad. I'll call Detective Loveless and let him know what we know. Maybe they can help. We've only got a couple of more sets to make, let's finish up," Tuck said as he pulled his feet out of the mud with a sucking sound. At least the Made-In-Somewhere-Else snake boots didn't leak.

CHAPTER 13

"Hey Al, I've got Lieutenant Tucker on the phone! Pick up line two," Teddy Loveless said across the desk to his partner.

Al picked up the phone and said, "Hello Lieutenant, it's good to hear from you. What's up?"

"Hello Al, I've got something going on down here that might be related to our old case, and I thought that maybe you should know about it," Tuck replied.

Teddy spoke first while Al listened, "What have you got Tuck?"

"You know those prints that I had Ike send up yesterday? The girl, Courtney Wells, turned up murdered this morning with three small caliber holes in the back of her head!" Tuck said.

Both detectives sat bolt upright in their chairs at the news. Teddy continued with Tuck while Al took notes, "Tuck, tell me anything that you can about this girl, and the man that she was with. We have a John Doe with the same wounds up here, only he has been dead since about the time that your wife got out of the hospital. I think that we may see if Myrtle Beach will invite us down for a look-see."

"I appreciate you guys. There is not much to tell about the killer. He seemed to have no features that stood out as far as I can recall. Call me when you get here so we can have a bite before you go back," Tuck sounded relieved that the men were going to check on the case.

"Tuck, if ballistics confirms that this is the same killer, we will be there, and we will take you up on something to eat! Thanks for calling us on this," Teddy ended the call, "Well Al, what you think?"

"Like you said, it depends on the ballistics, but if this is our killer, and he is following Tuck, that boy is in a lot of danger."

"My thoughts exactly, Al, let's go get something to eat, and then I'll call Myrtle Beach for a ballistics report," Teddy said as he started for the door. He turned back to Al who was slow in getting up, "Al, what if this is part of that conspiracy? We probably should let Captain Grays know."

"Good idea, Teddy, right after dinner!" Al replied as he dug in his jacket pocket for another Rolaids.

"Detectives, I want you both to tread very lightly on this case. If there is any hint of a connection to that conspiracy, I want it to be reported to me only, am I understood?" Captain Grays addressed the men behind the closed door of the office, "How soon can we have the ballistics from Myrtle Beach?"

"Teddy made the call a few minutes ago, so it may be an hour or so before we get the pictures of the slugs for comparison. They haven't entered them into the FBI database yet, so it will have to be a visual match in our lab," Al responded.

"Good! As soon as we have a match, if we have a match, I want you men to head for Myrtle Beach. I'll make the necessary calls to put you in the lead down there. For the time being, let's leave the FBI out of the loop, but time is of the essence. This killer is after someone or he wouldn't be tailing Lieutenant Tucker. I want him stopped before that man or his family is hurt or killed, understood?" Captain Grays stood up, signaling dismissal.

"Yes, sir!" Both men said simultaneously as they left the room and returned to their desks. Al had a new email waiting.

"Hey, this is from Myrtle Beach! I'll bet it is the ballistic pictures," Al said as he opened the mail, "Teddy, how about pulling up a print of our slugs, and we can compare them. Those boys in the Sun/Fun capital really work fast!"

Teddy printed out the pictures of the slugs that were taken from the victim in the manure pile, and they headed to the lab to do the comparison.

"Shirley, can you take a look at these slugs for us?" Teddy said as they walked into the crime lab.

Shirley, the outgoing lady that ran the forensics department looked up from her desk and greeted them, "Hi Teddy, Al, sure just lay them down over there and I'll get right on them. It shouldn't take but a minute."

Shirley walked over to a comparator that she used and loaded the photos in the viewport. After what seemed like an hour, but was only a few minutes, Shirley spoke, "Well, guys, the bullets were definitely fired from the same gun. Judging by the lack of deformation in our samples and those of this other photo, I'd say that they were probably a sub-sonic load. If so, then a mildly suppressed handgun would make no detectable sound, even fairly close to the muzzle. Was I helpful?"

"Shirley, we owe you dinner!" Teddy exclaimed, "Just name the date."

The Detectives left the room to Shirley's, "Okay, I'm going to hold you to that, Teddy Loveless!"

As Al and Teddy made their way to Captain Gray's office, Al said to Teddy, "If this is connected to our conspiracy, then who is the John Doe in the morgue? I think that we need to follow up on the people that were interviewed and check on their locations."

"Since that Andrew Ploughman character bonded out until his hearing, there is only Ralph Warren. As soon as we are finished with the Captain, I'll check on him," Teddy replied.

"Come in Detectives!" Captain Gray called out before they knocked, "I assume we have a match?"

"Yes sir, we have a match. The killer of our John Doe is the same as the man that was spying on Lieutenant Tucker and the killer of the escort in Myrtle Beach," Al spoke up, "We want to check our John Doe against the people that we know to be involved here in Columbia before we head to Myrtle Beach if that is okay with you."

"Absolutely, but I would reiterate that urgency is required if we are going to stop another killing. If you hit a dead end down there, call the local FBI in on this, but wait until it is absolutely necessary, understand?" Captain Grays replied, "Oh, you had better call the Lieutenant and put him on notice. It won't hurt for him to be on alert."

"Yes, sir," and the two men left the office.

CHAPTER 14

As the rain gradually stopped, and the air started drying out, the smell from the baited traps began wafting through the air, eventually coming to the nose of the alpha female as she led a pack of six coy-wolves in the pursuit of game. It didn't take long for her to find one of the buckets with the number two conibear trap just inside the hole that had been cut in the top. The smell of the chicken parts that were in the bottom of the bucket, which was lying on its side, was too much temptation for the female coyote that was nursing another litter of pups. Growling a warning at the others that were advancing on the bucket, she stuck her head in the hole. The trap closed shut with a loud snap around her neck, killing her almost instantly. As her legs jerked in her death throes, the others ran away from the scene toward a new source of scent and were soon hanging by their mouths with their legs not quite touching the ground, as Harry's turtle hook sets proved deadly to the young coy-wolves.

The rest of the pack was ranging close by with the big coy-wolf alpha male in the lead. He soon discovered another bucket trap and sniffed at it to investigate the aroma coming from inside. Something did not seem quite right to him so he growled a warning at the others and walked away into the brush. The pack followed, but one of the coyotes turned back and stuck his head inside to get the chicken. The noise of the trap and the death throes of the coyote got the attention of the pack leader, and he ran back to the bucket in time to watch the last shudder of the hapless victim of Tuck's trap.

As the pack gathered close, the alpha male made a series of growls and yips as if signaling the others to leave the buckets alone.

His rounds brought him to the five coy-wolves, his offspring from several months ago, that were hanging from the tree branches by their mouths. He barked a warning at the pack to stay clear of the chicken on the hooks, and the rest of the coyotes ran yipping along the game trail, past the five. As he left the hook sets, a whiff of the scent of his alpha female mate came to him on the light breeze. Something was wrong, and he immediately dropped low to the ground and gave a warning growl to the pack that spread out as if ready for an attack. As he came to her body and slowly sniffed her, a mournful howl escaped from his lips, followed soon after by the eerie howling of the rest of the pack, lamenting the death of their leader's mate.

The mournful howling of the pack was not unnoticed by the cougar as she slowly made her way through the swamp, looking for a meal. The pack was moving away from her so she let her feline curiosity take over as she covered the ground toward where she first heard the coyotes howling. Soon she arrived at the dead body of the alpha female, and all of her senses went on alert for danger.

Suddenly she heard a low whimper coming from a dense section of undergrowth, and a low guttural growl started in her throat as she slowly stalked the maker of that whimper. There in front of her were the five coy-wolves just hanging by their mouths. The big cat listened for the sound of the pack, but it was getting farther and farther away from her and this opportunity to feed. She circled the five slowly, reaching out to stick a razor sharp claw into one every few seconds to make them twitch in agony. Tiring of her cat-like game she approached the largest of the coy-wolves and stood on her hind legs to secure a grip on its throat with her teeth. She pulled savagely down and tore the animal from the hook , and then finished it off and began to feed, all the while looking at her next meals twisting in terror on the end of the marlin wire.

CHAPTER 15

"Hello, Lieutenant," Joel Biggs answered his phone.

"Hello, Joel. Bob Pike, Harry Albright, and I just set some traps over in the area to the North of Russ Lake, close to where the Faraday boy was attacked last year. I want you to go back in there with them tomorrow and kind of keep an eye on things. I've got some business to attend to that will keep me away most of the day," Tuck said, "If you will, have Private Knowles stay with the dog hunters and keep them away from that area. We don't want any trouble caused by killing a couple of prize hounds."

"I understand sir. Call me if you need anything tomorrow," Biggs replied.

"Thanks, Private, I'll stay in touch during the day by cell phone, although the signal is pretty iffy over there. Good luck with the hunt," Tuck said as he ended the call.

Tuck turned to Bob and Harry who were cleaning up the mess from the bait in the shed, "Well, Biggs will go with you guys tomorrow. I'd kind of like for you to feel him out for me. He might open up and tell you things that he wouldn't say to me in the field. We need to know who is on our side if this all goes crossways again."

"Sounds like a plan, Tuck," Bob replied, "I'm looking forward to seeing if our traps had any luck. How about you Harry?"

I'd be willing to bet that we kill one or two coyotes at least, but the one that we want is the alpha female since she usually is the one that holds the pack together. Get her and there is a good possibility that the pack will scatter," Harry replied.

"As soon as I meet with Al and Teddy tomorrow and find out what they want to talk to me about, I'll come back here and let you know what we are up against. They were certainly secretive on the phone," Tuck finished with, "I'm going inside and help Hanna with dinner, so don't be long."

Al and Teddy arrived at the Myrtle Beach Police Station for their meeting with Detective Steve Rogers who greeted them as they walked into the building, "I'll bet you two are Detectives Banks and Loveless from Columbia," He said as he shook their hands, "I got the call a couple of hours ago that you were coming so I've made arrangements for us to go directly to the crime scene and then maybe something to eat afterward. Does that suit you guys?"

Teddy handed Detective Rogers a manila envelope, "That sounds great Detective. We appreciate the hospitality and hope that by combining evidence, we can solve this case quickly. Inside that envelope are our ballistics photos and the fingerprints that your killer left on a glass the night that the hooker was killed."

"You're kidding me!" Rogers replied in genuine amazement, "How did you find glasses in Columbia that this guy used?"

Al gave him a sour look and said, "No, he was following a friend of ours down here that had the presence of mind to collect the glasses from the table that this guy and the girl were using."

"Did he get a good look at him? None of the people that we've talked to can identify the person that they saw with the girl," Rogers said.

"I'm afraid that is the same thing that our friend told us. There is something so common about this guy that he fits every description. That's why we're here. We think that he is a professional and may be after a target locally. He probably used the girl for a cover, and then killed her to tie up any loose ends,"

Teddy's cell phone rang, "Excuse me a minute while I get this. Hello Shirley, what have you got for me...ah, us?"

"Teddy you know those samples that the boys picked up at Ralph Warren's old apartment that you wanted me to screen for DNA against the remains that we brought in the other night?" Shirley asked in a coy voice and then waited for Teddy to reply.

"Of course, I do Shirley. What did you find?" Teddy's curiosity was peaked.

"Well, you know that dinner that you owe me, Teddy? I want a steak dinner with all of the fixings added to the account! We have a match! Of course, this is just preliminary, but it certainly looks like our John Doe is Ralph Warren!" Shirley finished, her voice beaming.

"Make reservations, we'll go as soon as we get back, I promise!" Teddy replied as he ended the call.

Al and Detective Rogers were just staring at Teddy as he turned back to them. Teddy stopped for a second and then realized that they had only heard his side of the conversation, which sounded like he was setting up a date, "What? No, no, no, it's not like that. Shirley matched the DNA from our John Doe to that of Ralph Warren, at least tentatively. She still has more tests to run, but I think that it is safe to assume that this psycho that we are looking for is working for the same people that caused all of the trouble with those cougars!"

"Gentlemen, we need to work fast if we are going to get our hands on this guy, especially if he is still hunting someone in the area," Detective Rogers said, "Let's go to the motel, and then over to RIOZ. Maybe someone remembers what this guy looked like over there."

"Before we go, I need to use the men's room and get a cup of coffee. Have you got any Rolaids handy?" Al asked.

Teddy just looked at Detective Rogers and smiled as he said, "We're a couple of old desk jockeys that can't hold their water like you young fellows do. Give us a few minutes."

"Sure thing fellows, I'll be in my office over there when you are ready," Rogers replied, and walked into the area that he had indicated.

The motel had little in the way of evidence, except for an abandoned car that wasn't registered to anyone residing there, although one of the ladies thought that she saw Courtney get out of it the night that she was murdered. The clientele of the motel were mostly drifters and prostitutes, and no one had anything to add to what Detective Rogers had already gathered, except the information about the car.

"How about having that car impounded? We might get lucky and pull some prints," Al asked.

"I'll call that in right away, Al. Now let's go over to RIOZ and ask a few questions. Have you guys ever been there before?" Rogers asked.

"Nope, we're mostly late night Ernie's and the occasional Waffle House," Teddy replied with a laugh.

"Well, maybe I can get Henrique, the owner, to comp us a meal, if he is in," Rogers suggested as they returned to the car, "We'll have that car in the impoundment in a couple of hours. Our guys are pretty thorough, so maybe something will turn up by tomorrow. Hey, I just had a thought. When that attempt was made on Mrs. Tucker's life a few months back, we fingerprinted that truck that was used, but could never match the prints that we found to any database. I'd like to run those from the glass at RIOZ to the ones that we have on file. What if it is the same guy?"

Teddy and Al exchanged glances before Al answered, "Detective, we need to ask you to keep confidential what I am going to tell you."

"Sure, no problem as long as it isn't something illegal," Rogers answered.

"We think that this killer is hardwired to kill, even though the person that hired him is dead, and we think that he is going after Hanna Tucker again! The reason that we need to keep this quiet is that we don't know how deep the level of corruption within the FBI runs, but we know that it is there, and he might have contacts within that organization that will tip him off that we are on to him," Al explained.

"I'm in agreement guys," Rogers said as they pulled up to RIOZ and got out. When they entered the expansive lobby, Rogers showed his badge discretely to one of the hostesses and asked, "Could we possibly speak to Henrique, if he is not too busy?"

"Certainly sir, I'll go get him for you," The young girl replied.

Several minutes passed before Henrique arrived with a friendly greeting and a warm smile, "Hello Detective Rogers, how can I help you tonight?"

"Good evening, Henrique, these gentlemen are detectives from Columbia that are here to help me solve one of our local homicides. We were wondering if we might be able to talk to the gaucho that served this young woman two nights ago," Rogers asked while showing Henrique the photograph of Courtney Wells.

"Certainly you may, although I'm not certain exactly what area that she was seated in. Do you have any other information?" He asked.

"It was the night that Lieutenant Tucker asked for the glasses off the table where Miss Wells was seated," Teddy volunteered.

"Ah yes. I remember exactly now. I'll tell you what. It is very busy just now, but it should be slowing down in the next hour. Why don't you men have dinner on me, and we will deal with this afterward," Henrique offered.

"You are very gracious, my friend," Rogers replied, and he led Teddy and Al to the Hostess that waited to seat them.

After dinner, the men talked to the young man that had served Courtney Wells and her escort, and he remembered only one thing about the man that they were now hunting.

"His eyes looked like there was no one home," He told the detectives, "He was empty is all that I can say. I really don't know what he looked like other than that."

Rogers thanked the young man and Henrique for his generosity, and then the men walked to the car.

"Where are you staying tonight?" Rogers asked.

"We're at the Holiday Inn Express somewhere close to Broadway at the Beach," Teddy replied.

"It's right there," Rogers said pointing to the hotel as they drove by, "just drive straight back from the station and you'll be here in ten minutes. What is on the schedule tomorrow?"

"Well, if you get a match on those prints from the truck, how about checking the Interpol database. We only looked at the domestic files when we pulled them off the glass. We've got a meeting with Lieutenant Tucker at nine o' clock. We can meet at noon at the station if you would like," Al replied.

"Sounds like a plan gentlemen. Get a good night's sleep and I'll see you in the morning," Rogers said as he dropped them off at the station to pick up their rental car.

"Hey Al, have you ever seen so much food? I'm going to dream about quail eggs tonight!" Teddy said with a laugh as they drove to the hotel.

"All I can think of right now is buying another pack of Rolaids," Al replied with a sour expression on his face, "You know that we might not get to this guy in time, don't you Teddy? How are we going to tell that to Lieutenant Tucker?"

"If we just had a decent contact with the feds, I'll bet someone would recognize the M.O," Teddy replied as they pulled into the hotel parking lot, "Maybe Lieutenant Tucker has an idea. We'll cover that with him tomorrow."

CHAPTER 16

Tuck woke from a deep sleep to the sound of Weston growling at the back door of the house and swung his legs out of bed while reaching for the Rock Island Arsenal M-5, twelve-gauge riot gun that he had recently purchased for their home defense weapon of choice.

He made his way quietly to the door and whispered to Weston, "Keep it down boy; you are going to wake up Hanna!"

Weston kept pawing at the door to signal Tuck that he wanted a piece of whatever was out there.

"That raccoon is going to kick your big butt one of these days, but if you want to try him tonight, just keep it down a bit," With that, Tuck opened the door and let Weston out.

The big Labrador immediately ran to the heavy shrubbery across the back yard from the garage and started casting about for a scent of whatever had alarmed him. Tuck decided that as serious as Weston was searching, he had better take a look also so he stepped out of the back door and was bent over to retrieve a set of muddy boots to slip on his feet when the first of two small caliber rounds struck the window of the storm door where he had been standing a second before. The second round struck where he had been before rolling off the small raised stoop and presenting the shotgun in the direction of the small but distinct pop of the silenced weapon that had just been discharged. The third round struck Weston just above the eye as he charged the threat to his owner, killing him instantly, but giving Tuck a slight target as the minimized flash of the suppressed muzzle blast indicated the likely position of the enemy.

Tuck quickly loosed three rounds of double aught buckshot from the three inch, twelve gauge magnums in the shotgun directly to the left of the spot that he saw the flash, and was rewarded by a muffled cry as the shadowy figure of his attacker ran to escape along the fence line behind the shrubbery. Tuck immediately fired the last two rounds in the shotgun toward the running figure, and then ran toward the driveway while reloading the pump shotgun from the slip over shell holder on the buttstock. As he turned toward the street, Tuck heard the loud report of a .45ACP coming from the front of the house as Hanna turned loose eight rapid fire rounds from the Ruger P-90 in the direction of the killer's car as it sped by.

"Michael, are you all right?" was her first breathless question as Tuck rounded the corner of the house and ran toward his wife.

"I'm fine, Hon! Are you hit?" Tuck asked as he took Hanna in his arms and started back into the house.

"No, I don't think so. Whoever that was, seemed very determined to just get away. I heard the glass break on the back door and then the shotgun firing, so I just grabbed the pistol and headed to the front door. Tuck, where is Weston?" Hanna was responding to Tuck's question when she thought about the dog.

"I'm not sure, but I think that he may have been hit. The last round that our guest fired was not at me. You call 911 and report this and I'll go check on our boy," Tuck reply with a worried note in his voice as he hurried to the back door.

Tuck found Weston lying on his side at the edge of the shrubbery with a small hole just above his eye. With his eyes full of tears, he reached down and scratched the big mutt's head behind the ear for the last time.

"Well, old friend, you probably saved my life again, and for that I am grateful. I sure hope that a few of the squirrels that you have caught over the years have made it to where you are now because you certainly have earned a reward!"

Tuck turned at the sound of Hanna walking up behind him, and he got up and put his arms around here, "He's gone, Hon, but we need to leave him until the police get through with their investigation."

"Oh, Tuck, he was such a good dog. I am so angry right now that this could be happening to us. When is it going to be over?" Hanna said through her tears as waves of sadness washed over her.

As the first police officer responded to the call and pulled into the driveway, Tuck pulled Hanna closer and said, "I promise you that somehow, I will find a way to end this and protect you and our son, Hanna. We need to do like Harry says all of the time, 'Have faith in God' and pray!"

The second car to arrive with a screech of rubber in the front of the house was Ike's cruiser followed by what seemed to be the entire police force of Conway, South Carolina and all of the deputies of Horry County. Privates Junior Knowles and Joel Biggs were the last to arrive in their DNR trucks.

"Lieutenant Tucker, what happened?" was the first question that the young police officer asked as he ran up the drive toward the couple with his service pistol drawn.

"We had a visitor that tried to kill us, but my dog ruined his plans," Tuck responded as he pointed to the motionless body of the hero dog lying on the ground in front of them, "I think that I may have hit him, though," Tuck told the officer without taking his eyes off Weston's body, "He made a sound like some of the pellets caught him on the second shot, and I believe that he was standing over there about ten feet away from the dog," Tuck indicated an area in the azaleas next to a large yellow pine tree.

As the officer walked slowly to the spot that Tuck had indicated, sweeping the ground with his tactical light, Ike, Privates Biggs and Knowles came at a run around the house to where Tuck was standing in his pajama bottoms still holding his shotgun in his right hand.

"Hey fellows, I sure appreciate you all showing up tonight, but it is going to make for a long day tomorrow," Tuck said in a half joking manner.

"Never mind that Lieutenant, we just wanted to make sure that you and the missus were all right," Joel Biggs was the first to reply.

"Tuck, Hanna got some glass when that fellow drove by. I've got three deputies checking the street, and two female deputies are in the house with Hanna. Are you sure that you are okay?" Ike asked.

"I'm fine, Ike, just upset about Weston and more than a little concerned for Hanna's safety. Can you get someone to take her to Harry's for me?" Tuck responded.

"Sure Tuck, but you need to tell her that she is going because she will want to stay here and help find that fellow," Ike replied.

"Thanks, Ike. You are a good friend," Tuck said as he turned to Joel Biggs, "I'm going to need both of you to take over checking our coyote sets with Harry Albright and Bob Pike tomorrow since I'll be tied up for most of the day, so you need to go home and get some sleep. Joel, you will be in charge. I want everything else suspended until we get some positive results on both the coyote pack and the cougar."

"Yes, sir Lieutenant!" Joel Biggs responded as he and Junior Knowles turned to leave, then looking back over his shoulder, "We are glad that you are all right, sir."

Tuck gave them a smile and a tired wave of his hand. He started to comment when an excited shout rang out from the area the young officer was searching, "Hey, we've got blood over here!"

All of the men carefully made their way into the area behind the shrubbery and looked intently at the blood spatters that the officer was indicating with his light.

Joel Biggs was the first to comment, "Well, that is definitely from a muscle wound. It is too dark to be upper body so I'd say a leg hit."

Ike replied in agreement, "Yep, it looks like you hit him pretty hard too if he lost that much blood that fast. Do we have a trail?"

The officer knelt down and carefully put the leaves with the blood droplets into an evidence bag for testing, and then started looking around for more blood. Sure enough, the blood spatters continued all the way to the sidewalk, and to an area where the getaway car must have been parked.

"Tuck, we'll take over from here. Whatever the city doesn't cover, the county will, so we are going to catch this guy. Now go tell Hanna that she has to go to her Dad's," Ike said as he put his hand on Tuck's shoulder.

Tuck was just starting to answer when Maggie O'Brien and the cameraman from WLIB news came running up the drive. Ike had his back to the driveway, but Tuck could hear him mutter an expletive under his breath before he turned to greet the unwelcome but expected visitors.

"Hello, Miss O'Brien. We don't have a statement for you yet, and you need to move back down the drive until our forensics people mop up the scene."

Maggie ignored Ike and directed a question at Tuck, "Lieutenant Tucker, can you tell us what happened this morning?"

"Maggie, I'm going to have to side with Deputy Baumgarner on this. Hanna and I are in a bit of shock, but I promise that we will give you an exclusive interview as soon as it is safe for us to do so," Tuck responded.

Maggie angrily turned to walk back down the drive all the while recording what little she knew of the shooting for her six am viewers.

"Ike, I've had a change of heart. I'll take Hanna to Myrtle Beach in my truck if you can escort us. I'd like to get away from this for a few hours myself," Tuck spoke quietly to his friend, "Oh Ike, the police will probably want to take that bullet out of Weston so tell them that I want to bury his remains here on the property, will you?"

"I'll take care of everything, Tuck. Go on in and get ready to leave."

CHAPTER 17

"Hey Al, look at this breaking news report!" Teddy Loveless shouted at his partner as they took advantage of the free breakfast, which consisted mainly of bagels, donuts, cold cereal, juice, and coffee.

The men were silent as the news of the attack on Tuck and Hanna played out across the big screen TV in the lobby of the Holiday Inn Express where they had spent the night.

"Well, that bastard didn't wait long now did he?" Al declared rhetorically.

"We've got to go. This could be the break that we're looking for," Teddy declared as he stood up and gulped the last of his coffee.

Both men had already checked out, and their overnight bags were in the rental car that was parked outside in the loading area. Teddy turned to see Al coming behind him with two cups of coffee in his hand.

"Good thinking partner!" Teddy exclaimed, and then on a more somber note, "I wonder how the Lieutenant is going to react when we tell him that we knew this was going to happen?"

"We'll find out when you give him a call," Al responded as he dug into his pocket for a Rolaids, "Let's get to the station and see if Detective Rogers can give us some more information on the last night's attack,"

As they walked through the doors of the Myrtle Beach police station, they were surprised to see Detective Rogers talking to two men in suits that had the look of FBI all over them.

Rogers waved them over, "Good morning men, these are agents Rossi and Stewart from the Myrtle Beach office of the FBI, Agents, this is Detective Alvarez Banks and Detective Teddy

Loveless from Columbia. I believe we are all looking for the same man."

After the introductions were made, Detective Rogers ushered the four men into a conference room. Agent Rossi was the first to speak, "Because of the attack on Lieutenant Michael Tucker and his wife this morning, the FBI is going to take charge of any and all current investigations dealing with the person that we believe to be responsible. That includes any unsolved homicides that Columbia and Myrtle Beach may be working on. We have a team conducting a sweep of the Tucker residence now for any forensic evidence, and I want any other evidence that may have been gathered on these related cases to be turned over to us. Are there any questions?"

Al and Teddy exchanged a quick glance and then Teddy caught Roger's eye and gave him an almost imperceptible shake of his head.

"We understand perfectly Agent Rossi, and if we uncover anything it will be turned over immediately," Al spoke while getting to his feet and extending his hand to the FBI agent as a sign of compliance.

"Well, gentlemen, I guess that wraps it up," Detective Rogers said as he stood to signal the end of the meeting, "The FBI will have our total cooperation."

With that, the two agents shook hands all around and left the room.

"I hope that you two know that we can get into big trouble for withholding evidence from those guys, don't you?" Rogers asked nervously.

"Don't worry about us Detective, you need to worry that those clowns don't screw this up and get the lieutenant and his family killed. Have you got anybody on the team that can get us some of the evidence, like maybe a drop of blood or a bullet?" Al replied.

"I think so. There is a deputy sheriff named Ike Baumgarner that might be able to help," Rogers responded.

"We know the deputy from the last time we were down. You talk to him while we go see Lieutenant Tucker," Al finished and motioned for Teddy as he started for the door, "Oh, one more thing, detective; we are already set for our retirement, so you can make a big splash if we get ahead of the feds on this...if you catch my meaning."

"I do indeed! Check back in with me after lunch and we can compare notes," Rogers said with a big grin. He could already feel the promotion coming his way.

Tuck was waiting in the driveway of Harry's with Bob Pike when Al and Teddy pulled up. It was now almost nine am and Tuck looked tired.

"Hey guys, I sure glad to see you this morning. Come on in the house and get some coffee," Tuck greeted the two detectives as they got out of the car. He also took note of the plain tan Chevrolet that had parked around the corner in front of a vacant lot on the next street.

The two detectives shook hands with Tuck and Bob Pike, looked briefly in the direction of the Chevrolet, and then followed Tuck inside.

Teddy spoke first, "We want to apologize for not warning you last night that this guy might try to attack your wife again, Lieutenant. We didn't have much to go on but our gut instinct, but we should have called anyway."

"Attack Hanna, why do you think that she is the target?" Tuck sounded surprised.

"Just an educated guess I suppose, but the first victim that was killed around the time of the attempt on Mrs. Tucker was the roommate of that Jonathon Oakes, Ralph Warren. The ballistics and M.O. match the second victim, Miss Wells, and I'd bet that ballistics will prove that the same gun fired at you and killed your dog this morning," Al replied, "By the way, where is Mrs. Tucker?"

"Hanna is with her father and stepmom. They took her for a check-up this morning. Don't worry; they've got plenty of security surrounding them," Tuck said with a small smile. He was thinking about the friends that he had made in the law enforcement community that were now giving them around the clock protection, whether they wanted it or not, "Besides, we have our friends in the tan Chevy keeping an eye on us also, but probably for different reasons that are known only to whomever they answer to."

The men all nodded at the last comment and were silent for a second before Al spoke up, "Lieutenant, we want you to know that Teddy and I are going to stick on this case as long as we can. The feds are involved now so we have to be very discreet, but we will funnel as much information to you as we can. The more pressure that we can put on this loon, the more off balance he will be, and perhaps one of us will get lucky."

"Thanks, guys, I appreciate your help and everything that you are doing for us. Are you going back to Columbia today?" Tuck asked.

"We probably will leave just as soon as we get some pictures of that slug that they recovered from your dog. We sure are sorry about him getting killed. He was a beautiful animal," Teddy replied.

"Yes, he was," Tuck softly replied.

The men got up and moved to the door.

"Mr. Pike, I forgot to ask how you and the Missus were doing down in Honduras?" Al asked.

"Thanks for asking, Detective. We were doing all right, but we've missed home a bit. It seems that we are being shadowed there also," Bob replied.

"Well, give her our best when you get home," and with that, both men walked to their car and drove away.

"What do you think, Bob?" Tuck asked as he watched the car pull out of the driveway.

"I think we are going to have to hunt this guy ourselves, Tuck, or you'll never get another good night's sleep," Bob replied, "What we need now is a plan."

"Well, I'd better call Joel and let him know that it will be you and I checking the traps with him this morning. I always think better in the woods," Tuck responded with a smile, "Besides, Harry is going to be good security for Hanna, and I don't want her left alone."

CHAPTER 18

Joel Biggs had sent Jr. Knowles with the dog hunters into Northern section of the swamp above the power line, while he drove to the area where Tuck had set his traps to wait for Bob and Tuck to show up. As he got out of the truck and turned to reach into the back seat for his shotgun, a movement out of the corner of his eye caught his attention. Acting as if he had not noticed the intruder, Joel slowly worked the action of the 870 Remington and chambered a three inch, 4/0 buckshot cartridge, as he spun quickly in the direction of the shadowy figure and brought the shotgun to bear where the target was seen. For a brief instant, from a distance of thirty yards, the tawny face of an adult cougar was visible, and then the cat leapt gracefully and quickly into the tree line.

Tuck pulled up alongside Joel's truck just as Joel lowered his shotgun.

"What is it, Joel?" Tuck asked as he quickly pulled his shotgun from the rear seat of his truck, "You look like you've seen a ghost!"

"I might have, Lieutenant. There was a cougar stalking me when I got out of my truck!" Joel Biggs answered with a quaver in his voice. It was obvious to both Bob and Tuck that he had been shaken up by the brief encounter.

"Let's go over there and see if we can see any prints," Bob suggested. He was carrying Harry's FN FAL on the three-point sling.

The men eased over to the spot where the cougar had been standing and searched the area for tracks. Joel Biggs found the first one.

"Over here, Lieutenant," He called, "I've got a good print in this wet sand"

Bob squatted down and put his hand alongside the track, "Well, it isn't the size of Tuck's monster, but that is certainly a big cat that was planning on you for lunch, Joel. Judging from those other two we killed, I'd say around one hundred and eighty or ninety pounds."

"Let's get the bait out of the truck and go check our sets from yesterday. This cat has no fear of humans, so be very careful," Tuck told the two men.

As they got near the area where they had set the traps, Tuck and Bob made softball-sized balls of the mixture that Harry had concocted the day before.

"Man that stuff stinks!" complained Joel as he kept a wary eye on their surroundings. The visibility was limited to a dozen yards at the most, and the cat could be behind any of the many clumps of swamp grass or fallen trees.

"It might stink, but to any animal that licks his rear, it might smell like heaven," laughed Bob as he rolled up another ball of the deadly bait.

Tuck suppressed he urge to laugh as he dropped the last of the stink baits and peeled off his latex gloves.

"Let's go check those sets and see if we've had any luck," He said to the other two men as they finished up, "The first one should be about a hundred feet beyond that old cypress log," Tuck finished by pointing to a thick area along the game trail where an old cypress tree lay beside a stagnant pool of water.

The first bucket set was undisturbed so the men carefully eased down the trail toward the second set while keeping a watch for the cougar. The next bucket had been rolled away from the trail by the death throes of the alpha female of the pack. Tuck knelt down and removed the bucket lid so that he could release the trap springs.

"That is sure a healthy coyote, Tuck!" Bob exclaimed, "Do you think this could be the one we are after?"

"I don't know about that, Bob, but she's one less for us to worry about, that's for sure," Tuck said as he laid the carcass out and took a picture with his cell phone, "We'll get her on the way back so that Harry can see the fruit of our labors," Tuck said with a smile. He was trying to hide his concern for Hanna and her family while he was out here, but Harry was more than capable of handling most situations, provided that he could see it coming.

Joel Biggs had walked on toward the next bucket.

"Hey, we've got another one!" He shouted out as he knelt to remove the lid. Inside of the trap was a large young male coyote with a short snout.

"I think we have a wolf mix here, Lieutenant," Joel said as the others joined him.

"That's what I was afraid of," Tuck said as he looked at the body of the coy/wolf, "That will mean a more aggressive pack, and probably a larger one if the alpha is also a wolf mix."

Bob Pike had carefully and quietly moved along to the next bucket, which was undisturbed. As the other two came up behind him, Bob moved on up the trail to the next bucket.

"Holy Crap!" he exclaimed as he jumped back about three feet. "Tuck, you've got to see this!"

The three men stood and looked in amazement at the four feet of cottonmouth that was hanging outside of the bucket lid, its body still twitching.

"I think that we should leave that one alone until he's finished moving," Bob said, "I hate snakes!"

"I'm not real fond of them myself, Bob, but you've got to admit, that is a real beauty as moccasins go," Tuck said with a grin. Joel Biggs just shook his head and smiled as they walked past the bucket, each man giving the body of the snake a wide berth.

As they approached the small clearing that had been ringed with the hook sets, Joel gave a soft whistle and crouched down. There were remains scattered about under the hooks and it was obvious that a very large cat had been on a killing spree here.

"It looks like we got another five here, but judging from this track, our cougar found them while they were still hanging," Joel said to Tuck as he came up crouched down beside of him.

"Tuck, Harry, and I set two more buckets further in toward the lake while you were on the way back to the truck. I think we should probably pull them back and use the chicken to reset these hooks. It will certainly be good stink bait by now. That pack may run back through here tonight, and we can catch another stupid one or two," Bob said.

They walked toward the final bucket sets with Bob Pike leading the way when suddenly the scream of an enraged cougar erupted from an area just beyond the last bucket. All three men reacted to the immediate threat in unison with Joel dropping into a semi-kneeling position, shotgun extended toward the sound and Tuck moving to the left for a better view.

"Why is that cat in here where we are, Bob?" Tuck whispered.

"It sure seems rather odd, doesn't it? We need to be very careful," Bob replied. He held the FN at the ready as he slowly made his way toward the first bucket.

The other two were fanned out now, flanking Bob with their shotguns at the ready and every nerve on edge.

"This one is empty!" Bob exclaimed as he eased past the first bucket.

"That one has been moved," Bob said as he reached the last set, the lid of which was turned away from him. As he reached the bucket, a low growl came from a thick growth of brush to their left and about fifty yards from where they were standing.

"I've heard that before!" Tuck exclaimed between clenched teeth as he turned to face the threat.

Bob reached the bucket and saw what was trapped. "You need to see this!" he exclaimed to the others, "We've got a cougar kitten in this one!"

The growl turned into a scream of rage as Bob knelt to open the trap. Sensing an attack was imminent, Tuck fired two rounds of four-aught buck at the shrubbery where the cat was hiding, and the screaming stopped abruptly.

"Work fast, Bob. I'm going over there and see if I made a lucky shot. Joel, stay with Bob and help him get that cat back to the truck. We'll deal with the buckets later," Tuck gave his orders while he slowly moved toward the spot that had held the female cougar.

"Yes, sir!" Joel exclaimed, and then to Bob, "Swap guns with me so I can cover him."

Bob handed the FN to Joel who then took a shooting stance using a cypress for a steady rest. Tuck reached the brush and made a wide circle of the thick area, looking carefully for any sign of movement before going in, but the cougar had fled at the sound of the shotgun pellets tearing into the vegetation. Tuck came back into view of the men and gave them a hand warning to look behind them as they left the area. He then moved to a position slightly behind Bob and Joel Biggs so that he could cover their rear. One thing that he knew was that the cougar was not going to leave her kitten without following them out.

Joel stooped to recover the female coyote carcass and kept his shotgun at the ready in his right hand, his eyes stayed on the area to their backs as Tuck brought up the rear. All three of the men's nerves were frayed to the snapping point as they cleared the last of the tree line when suddenly the fearsome scream of rage from the mother of the kitten sounded from a few yards inside of thick foliage.

Tuck spun to face the threat and dropped to one knee while bringing the shotgun to bear on the area that the sound emanated from.

"Get everything in the truck, private, and then give me cover," He whispered an order at Joel Biggs.

Biggs and Bob Pike tossed the remains of the two animals into the back of the truck and Joel turned to face the threat.

"We're ready Lieutenant," He said quietly.

Tuck backed to the truck, never taking his eyes off the tree line, and Joel Biggs backed to the passenger side in the same manner.

As the men shut the truck doors the sound of the enraged cougar penetrated the cab of the truck, but she did not show herself.

Tuck turned the truck out into the middle of a clear cut about fifty yards from the tree line, and then spoke to the confused look on Bob and Joel's faces.

"Gentleman, we need to kill that cat!"

With that, he shut the truck off and got out. Bob and Joel looked at each other and then followed suit.

Tuck signaled to the others to spread out and enter the woods at intervals of fifty feet as they advanced toward the spot where the last scream had come from.

"Shoot to kill, men," Tuck said with determination as they entered the heavy brush of the tree line.

CHAPTER 19

As Harry Albright stood quietly in the grotto of the Pirate's Cove Putt Putt golf course, he watched the waterfall on either side of the room where the meeting with Agent Morris would take place. The sound that the vibrant blue-green water made as it cascaded softly over the artificial mountain would serve well to hide a conversation and Harry knew that it had been carefully selected. An older woman and her grandson played on past Harry as he waited, followed by a young couple that seemed to be having the time of their lives as they gave Harry a big smile and a warm greeting as they played the grotto, and then departed.

"Hello Harry," the voice startled him as Anthony Morris slipped quietly into the grotto.

"Agent Morris, I'm afraid that you gave me a start," Harry said with a smile as he extended his hand in a greeting.

"Call me Anthony, Harry. I've come a long way down in the last few months," Anthony Morris replied as he shook Harry's hand.

"Okay, Anthony, just what is this meeting about? I have a hard time believing that we are just socializing over a game of Putt Putt here at Pirate's Cove," Harry replied.

"Well, for starters, your daughter and son-in-law are still in danger, Harry. The biggest threat is from some secretive wing of the Department of Natural Resources, but there is a serious threat to their liberty from within my own organization. Lieutenant Tucker really pissed some folks off when he and Bob Pike killed those rogue agents, not to mention giving the Bureau a very black eye in the process. My men shooting that one at your place got me demoted to agent status and pulled off your case," Anthony said as he quietly gave Harry the details.

"Well, I'm sure that you wouldn't have arranged this meeting if you didn't have a plan, Anthony. You do have a plan, don't you?" Harry asked after a brief pause.

"The Bureau has some very good people in its ranks, Harry, even though it is hard to stick to our patriotic beliefs with all of the pressure from Washington. I've arranged for Lieutenant Tucker and his wife, Bob Pike and his wife, and you and your wife to change identities and go into hiding…disappear if you will. I can provide finances, passports, and a couple of good locations where it would be unlikely that any of you would ever be found."

Harry was silent for a minute and then responded, "I can't speak for anyone but Kathryn and me, but the thought of leaving our congregation, and my other daughters and grandchildren is not acceptable to me."

"Harry, if they accept this offer of help and you don't, you can never see them again. Am I clear on that? They will have to be dead to you!" Anthony replied firmly.

"I understand Anthony, but the real concern needs to be for Tuck, Hanna, and the baby now. Do you have a timetable of when the danger to them will be the greatest?" Harry asked.

"Well, we know that based on the attack the other night, the man that tried to kill Hanna is still hunting her, and I think that my organization could move at any time to start a harassment campaign against the Lieutenant. I would guess that within the next thirty days, they would need to disappear. I realize that this is a hard thing to hear, but it is the best that I can do. Can you convey the urgency to them for me? I will arrange a meeting in a few days with all of the involved parties and get the response," Anthony said as he extended his hand to signal an end to the discussion.

Harry took his hand and said, "Of course."

Anthony Morris smiled and walked out of the grotto into the sun while Harry waited another ten minutes before leaving by the other side exit.

Hanna sat at Kathryn's kitchen table and talked as her stepmother fixed them a glass of tea.

"I know that Tuck can take care of himself, Kathryn, but I am frightened that this guy will get through and hurt my baby and me. I've never been this scared before," Hanna poured out her feelings to her stepmother.

"Harry and I have been praying that Godly wisdom will prevail in any decision that you two make, Hanna. We also think that it would be a good thing if you and Tuck moved in here for a couple of weeks until they catch the guy that tried to kill you," Kathryn replied.

"Sometimes I wish that we could just disappear and forget all of this. I really thought that everything was perfect until I woke up in that hospital room. All of this now seems like a very bad dream, and I can't wake up," Hanna spoke softly with tears running down her cheeks.

"God always has a plan, Hanna. We need to keep praying, but I know in my heart that there is a bright spot in the dark clouds coming soon for all of us," Kathryn responded as she put her arms around Hanna and comforted her, then, "I hear your father coming. Dry your eyes, and let's see what happened with Agent Morris."

CHAPTER 20

Like most animals that have lost their offspring, the cougar was torn between rage for the men that had taken the body of her kitten, and the urge to take him back. As she moved swiftly and silently through the swamp bottom ahead of her hunters, the big cat started moving in a circle that would bring her back to the opposite side of the clearing where her dead offspring lay in the back of the DNR Ford. One of Tuck's shotgun pellets had entered her right front foreleg and was lodged painfully in the opposite side just under the skin, slowing her down somewhat, but not enough for her to be overtaken by the men that were intent on killing her.

She found a thicket with a large cypress dead fall and crouched silently to observe her pursuers as they passed some fifty yards behind her before continuing deeper into the swamp toward Russ Lake. When they were out of sight, she made straight for the truck in long flowing strides and cleared the bed rails in one fluid move. Taking the dead kitten gently in her teeth by the nape of his neck, the mourning cat jumped from the opposite side of the truck and headed away from Russ Lake toward the woods of the Big Pee Dee River.

"Lieutenant, I think that we've lost her," was the matter of fact assessment of Joel Biggs after the three men had searched the soft edges of Russ Lake for signs that the cat had run through there.

"I have to agree with Joel," Bob added, "we will need some more men in here if we are going to kill this cat."

"Okay, let's wrap up tonight and get those carcasses back to the lab. We can get some men out here tomorrow if the weather holds," Tuck agreed as they headed back to the truck, although he couldn't help but notice that he wasn't the only one that was keeping a close eye on every clump of swamp grass big enough to hide the cougar.

Joel Biggs crossed the sandy road before the other men were out of the wood line, and as he looked down at the big paw print in the sand, he shouted for Tuck, "Over here Lieutenant, hurry!"

Tuck and Bob jogged the last yards over to Joel and looked in amazement at the cougar tracks that crossed the boot prints that they had just made!

"Holy Crap, she went straight for the truck!" Joel shouted as he ran to the vehicle and looked in the back.

"The kitten is gone!" he exclaimed, "It looks like Momma came back for her baby."

"Well, we missed a great opportunity by not sitting up on this one," Tuck said with disgust, "Let's head in. We can try this again tomorrow."

As the men loaded into the truck and slowly drove away, they failed to see the cougar lying in the brush, watching their departure with a low growl emanating from her throat. As soon as they were gone from view, she turned to nuzzle the cold and lifeless body of her kitten before pulling a pile of dirt and leaves over his remains.

CHAPTER 21

Special Agent Douglas Kensey leaned back at his desk with his hands folded behind his head and a smile on his face as he considered the pace at which he was moving up the FBI's ladder of success. Douglas Kensey was an ambitious young man with aspirations of becoming a key player in the Department of Justice even if it meant stepping over his fellow agents or obeying instructions that were beyond the scope of the acceptable protocol. He certainly wasn't like that Anthony Morris character that he had replaced and held in absolute contempt. In Douglas' mind, Morris had too much compassion for people to be effective in this job, an attribute that certainly was perceived as a weakness by some of the people that Agent Morris had answered to. The agency had lost some of their key black ops people under Morris's watch, and they were not about to have a repeat of those failures as long as Douglas Kensey was in control of the Myrtle Beach office, and the Michael Tucker case. This could be the one that moved him to Washington, and there was no way that a mere wildlife resources officer was going to stand in the way of this FBI agent clawing his way up the ladder.

Kensey's reverie was suddenly interrupted by his cell phone ringing, and he answered it with an irritated tone in his voice, "Yes, yes, what is it?"

"Sir, you told me to call your cell if we found something unusual going on," the voice on the other end said, "Albright just had a meeting with Agent Morris."

"Well, what was the meeting about?" Kensey asked sharply.

"We don't know, sir, they met in the grotto of a miniature golf course, and the waterfall noise masked their conversation."

"For Pete's sake, you know that I don't like incompetence! Find out what that meeting was about, and do it quickly. Do you understand?" Kensey was furious. His reputation and advancement hinged on getting enough evidence on Tucker and his family to tie them to the disappearance of Lawrence Richards, and his bodyguards, even if that evidence had to be fabricated. Morris would have to be dealt with, but that would be better off left to the powers-that-be in Washington for the present.

Special Agent Kensey looked through his cell phone contact list until he found the number that he wanted, and then placed the call with an evil smirk on his face.

"Biggs here," answered the voice on the other end of the call, then, "I can't talk right now," The phone went dead.

"Girl problems, Joel?" Tuck asked with a laugh as Joel Biggs put the phone back in his pocket.

Biggs forced a grin, "Yeah, I'll have to straighten it out later tonight."

Bob Pike was in the back seat of the truck and had caught a glimpse of the phone when it had shown the caller id. Whatever Biggs had going on did not have anything to do with a romance. He would tell Tuck at their earliest opportunity, but for right now, he just laughed as if he believed the lie that Joel Biggs had told Tuck. Whatever else he might be, Biggs was now the face of the enemy, and quite possibly a very deadly threat to all of them. Bob's mind turned to Abigail and the fact that he had left her alone in Honduras while he had come back here for the fundraising venture. A smile crossed his face as he thought of the surprise that anyone would get if they messed with Abby while he was gone!

Tuck dropped Joel Biggs at his truck, and then he and Bob drove to Myrtle Beach to see Hanna and the Albrights. On the way down, Bob broke the news to Tuck.

"Tuck, we have a big problem," he started, "Biggs is working with the FBI! I saw that Special Agent Kensey's name on his caller id when that call came in from his 'girlfriend'!"

"What? Are you certain?" Tuck asked in amazement.

"Yep, I saw the name Kensey as clear as day when that phone rang. Why else would he lie about a girlfriend if he wasn't working for the other side?" Bob replied.

Tuck was silent for a few minutes, and just sat there slowly shaking his head.

"Do you think that maybe you should head back to Honduras, Bob? Abby might need you before this is all over."

"No, Abby is in good hands," Bob replied with a smile, "I ran into an old friend of mine that used to live in Georgetown before retiring down there. He is looking after things in a quiet way until I get back; although I kind of wish that he was up here with us."

Tuck just looked at Bob and wondered what else he didn't know about his friend.

Douglas Kensey suddenly sat straight up in his chair. The thought, "Divide and Conquer!" raced through his mind as a plan began to form. He would separate Tuck from his friends, starting with Bob Pike, and what better way to do that than to have Pike rush back to La Ceiba to take care of his wife?

A quick shout to his secretary took care of the details; the rest would be sorted out on the flight over, "Donna, get me on the next flight to La Ceiba, Honduras, first class, and reserve me a quiet room down there."

"Yes sir," was the reply from the next room.

Now, all that was left to do would be to assemble a team. He knew that they had two men tailing Mrs. Pike, but Kensey wanted another four men on the ground in case any of his plans went wrong.

"You can't have too much backup!" he said to no one in particular as he made the necessary calls. By this time tomorrow, some of the loose ends would be wrapped up, and Very Special

Agent Douglas Kensey would be one rung closer to the top of the ladder. Yes, sir, life was starting to look good, very good indeed!

CHAPTER 22

"Hey, Al, ballistics have confirmed the gun that shot the Lieutenant's dog belongs to our mystery man! Shirley is running an analysis on the blood sample that we scored also," Teddy was returning to his desk and couldn't wait to tell his partner the good news.

"Well, where does that put us?" Al asked when Teddy had gotten seated, "We are up here in Columbia, and that psycho is on the loose in Myrtle Beach."

"Well, maybe we can get a DNA match and put a name and face on this guy. I sure would like to beat the Feds to this one," Teddy responded with a grin.

They were interrupted by the phone ringing on Teddy's desk. "Hey, Shirley, what have you got? Really, I'll be right down!" Teddy hung up the phone and gave Al a big grin.

"We have a name and a face! Let's go down to the lab!"

Al and Teddy practically ran down the two flights of stairs rather than wait on the elevator in their excitement over Shirley's news.

"Teddy, did you tell Shirley not to let anyone know that we had that blood or the bullets? I don't want the feds stealing our thunder on this," Al wheezed as he slowly regained his breath.

"Relax Al, Shirley is on the ball with this, and she won't let anything out until we give her the word," Teddy reassured him.

Shirley was waiting for them with a manila folder when they arrived in the lab, "Take this and hurry out of here. I've just gotten a phone call from a friend of mine over at the FBI that two agents are on the way to confiscate our evidence! Now Hurry!"

Teddy grabbed the envelope with one hand and hugged Shirley in passing, "Thanks, Shirley, we really owe you one!"

"Yes you do, more than one in fact, and I am not about to forget it! Now hurry, those guys are probably in the building by now!"

Al and Teddy hurried out the back door of the lab into the small alley behind the station. They needed to find a place to go over the information that Shirley had handed them before the FBI confiscated that also.

"I think that it is time to make a run to Ernie's, partner. What do you think?" Al asked.

"I think that the Feds are probably watching our car. Mine is just up the street and should be safe. We need to move!" Teddy responded.

With that, the two heavyset men almost ran the block and a half to Teddy's tired old Chevrolet wagon and threw themselves into the front seat. Teddy pulled out into the sparse late night traffic and immediately got off the main drive and onto the side streets for their getaway.

"Al, pull the batteries from our phones real quick," Teddy said as he handed Al his cell phone, "I may just be paranoid, but those guys have the technology to follow us if those things are powered up."

Al was still out of breath from the jog to the car, but he removed the batteries as Teddy had asked. Finally, he got his wind back enough to speak, "Teddy, head up to Blythewood. There is a McDonalds up there that is open all night, and we will be far enough out that these guys won't find us until we get back."

"Good idea, now how about looking through the file while we ride?" Teddy replied.

Al picked the folder up off the seat beside him and pulled a small tactical light from his jacket pocket. He scanned the papers for several minutes before speaking, "Teddy, we have to get word to the Lieutenant about what is in here. Find us a Wal-Mart so we can pick up a burner phone."

"There is one on the way. What is in there anyway?" Teddy responded to the urgency in Al's voice.

"Our psycho is an FBI wet boy by the name of George Withers. Apparently he went off the reservation after Richards was killed. I'm not liking what we've got ourselves into here, but the only way out is to catch this guy, and make it a public spectacle." Al had a worried tone in his voice that was out of character for the big man.

The stop at Wal-Mart produced a cell phone that they activated in the parking lot once they had returned to their car. Teddy had the burner number that Tuck had given to him in the case that an emergency call needed to be made so they decided to wake him up with the bad news.

"Hello," the sleepy voice answered the other phone.

Lieutenant Tucker, it's Detectives Loveless and Banks. We need to talk urgently," Teddy spoke.

"Hey guys, what in the world is going on at this hour?" Tuck was awake now and his senses were sharp.

"The man that hurt your wife and murdered those other people is an FBI assassin named George Withers. We have a picture of him that we will scan and fax to you in the next few minutes. An FBI team is looking for this information right now so we don't have a whole lot of time," Teddy filled Tuck in on what they had.

Okay, men. Harry has a fax machine here in his office. I'll go in there and get the number for you. Hold on for a minute," Tuck hurried out of the bedroom and down the hall to Harry's office with Hanna right behind him.

"843-555-1212 guys, I'm standing by," Tuck finished and ended the call.

"What is going on Michael? Are we in danger?" Hanna was frightened.

"No more than usual, Darling. Al and Teddy have got a lead on the jerk that tried to kill us, and they are sending a picture to me, that's all," Tuck reassured her as he gave her a big hug.

They waited for ten minutes before the fax machine started to ring. By this time Bob, Harry, and Kathryn had joined them in the study and watched as the documents started coming out of the printer.

"Tuck, we should make copies of these and get them into separate envelopes, just in case," Harry suggested, "I think that you should make a call to Ike as soon as possible also and let him know what you've got."

"Harry has a good point, Tuck," Bob pitched in, "We don't know how deep this goes into the FBI, but I'll bet that they will be hard on your friends in Columbia when it gets out that we know who their hit man is. Hell, for that matter, the knowledge that they have a hit man operating down here, regardless of who sent him, will cause a real problem for them."

"I'm going to wake Agent Morris up with this one," Harry said, "We are going to need all of the help we can get from this point forward, and Anthony Morris has already put his career on the line for us at least twice. You all know that this is the time that he was referring to when he said we would have to disappear, don't you? It certainly has come a lot sooner than he expected."

"Harry, Hanna and I are not going into hiding. You've been teaching me for a couple of years now about faith, and we think that it time for us to act like we have some," Tuck spoke for both he and Hanna. They and Bob had been briefed by Harry soon after Tuck returned to Myrtle Beach after the hunt. Along with Harry, the entire family unanimously decided to pass on the offer of witness protection, and Tuck spoke the thought that each of them had.

"I'm proud of you both, more than you can know," Harry said softly to Tuck and Hanna after Tuck's declaration, "We'll know tomorrow if anything else remains to be done, in the meantime, pray like you never had before."

As if a signal had been given, everyone quietly returned to their rooms...if not to sleep.

"Hey guys, where in the world have you been? The Feds are looking for you, and the Captain is having a fit," The young uniformed officer greeted them as they passed in the entry to the precinct house.

Al turned to Teddy and said in a very somber tone, "Well, let's go flush our retirements down the drain, Partner."

They walked slowly into the squad room and made it almost to the Captain's office before the two FBI agents confronted them. Almost simultaneously, Captain Grays stepped out of the office and motioned to the four men to step inside.

"Where in the hell have you men been for the last two hours?" he asked with a bark in his tone.

"We just went to get something to eat and lost track of time," Teddy offered half-heartedly.

The senior agent said, "We need the evidence that you two left the building with, and I mean immediately! Is that clear?"

"Absolutely, sir, I have it on my desk," Al responded. Unseen by the agents, Al had tossed the folder on his desk where it sat as if it had never left the building. He had been in this business much longer than the two 'wet behind the ears' agents combined, and he knew that unless he was holding the folder, they could not prove that it had left the building in their possession.

Captain Grays barked an order to one of the officers in the outer room, and the folder was handed to him momentarily, and then immediately turned over to the agents who stood there with embarrassed looks on their faces.

"Well, gentlemen, if that is all, these men have cases to work on," The Captain dismissed the two red-faced agents and closed the door behind them.

He turned to Al and Teddy and just stared at them for a very long and unnerving minute before asking, "Well, did you at least look at that damned file before you tossed it on the desk?

Teddy gave him a big smile and responded triumphantly, "Better than that, Sir. We copied it!"

He reached into his inner jacket pocket and retrieved the folded papers that contained the bulk of the report that the Feds had been so desperate to retrieve, and then handed them to Captain Grays, who received them with an astonished look on his face.

"Just when I thought that there was nothing new that you two couldn't pull off, you continually amaze me. Not a word of this to anyone, understand?" With that, he turned to his desk and proceeded to study the report that he had been handed. Al quietly led the way out of the office and back to their desk, closing the door behind them.

Teddy was the first to speak, "I guess that we'll just have to wait this one out now, Al."

"I suppose we will, Teddy. Have you got any Rolaids? All of this stress is cranking up my heartburn again," Al replied with a sour look on his face.

CHAPTER 23

From the moment that Douglas Kensey's flight touched down at the Goloson International Airport in La Ceiba, he was not alone. The flight had arrived at just after midnight, and Kensey failed to notice the large older gentleman that watched his every move from the shadows of the small terminal building.

As he made his way through the sparse crowd to the luggage area, Special Agent Kensey saw a tall dark skinned man with a very pocked mark face holding a cardboard sign with the name Douglas Kensey written in magic marker.

Kensey grabbed his one checked through bag and walked over to the man with the sign.

"Agent Kensey?" the man asked in poor English.

"Yes, and you are?" Kensey asked impatiently. He was used to being in absolute control of his men, and this would be no exception.

"I am Agent Regino Gonzales, at your service, sir," Regino answered.

"Good! How far is it to the hotel Elestadio? I am very tired and would like to get some sleep before briefing everyone involved in the morning," Kensey asked curtly.

"We are only a few miles from the hotel. Four of the men are also staying there and awaiting your arrival," was the response as Regino took the small bag from Kensey's shoulder and then picked up the larger bag from the floor, "The car is waiting at the curb."

The ride to the hotel was uneventful and quiet; quiet that is until they pulled up in the front of the somewhat garishly decorated, yellow, multi-story hotel with full balconies that just screamed, "BUDGET TOURIST LODGINGS"! Kensey took one look at the hotel and broke into a loud and lengthy tirade against third world hotels and the cheapskate bastards that he felt allowed them to exist through their patronage. When he got home, his secretary would get a piece of his mind before she joined the ranks of the under-employed in Myrtle Beach!

Regino listened to the tirade without any response and took the luggage from the car to the front desk as Special Agent Kensey followed, still breathing epitaphs against the hotel and Hondurans in general. When they arrived at the desk, he politely took his leave with, "Until tomorrow, Special Agent Kensey."

The tired and obviously irritated desk clerk managed to keep his composure through the ordeal of checking the thoroughly obnoxious American in, and, in a manner of peaceful protest, assigned Kensey a very small room on the third floor. To add insult to injury, he also explained in broken English that the elevator was out of order until a maintenance man could look at it in the morning, so Kensey had to trudge the stairs with his bag by himself. The room was painted a cantaloupe orange in color, but it was clean. The small full sized bed sat in a corner of the melon colored room, and a small refrigerator sat across from the bed. He looked into the tiny bathroom and saw the tub that doubled as a shower, along with the toilet, and a freestanding sink. The door to the balcony was broken so that it would not open, and the air conditioner wasn't working. While the air in the room was very still, the evening temperature had dropped into the sixties making the prospect of sleep not as bleak as it had seemed a few minutes before.

"If all goes well, I'll be out of this dump by tomorrow evening," Kensey said out loud just before he lay down on the bed and drifted off into a restless sleep filled with strange dreams from which he couldn't seem to wake.

When he was safely asleep, one of the shadows moved out of its place of hiding and approached the bed. Swiftly the big, rough looking older man inserted a needle into the jugular of the sleeping man, injecting a dose of Phenobarbital Sodium directly into Kensey's blood stream.

He then pocketed the syringe and opened the door of the small room, letting in two other men.

"Hey, Shaun, we thought that you'd retired. Did you get bored with the salvage operation up in the Carolinas? Is that the guy that you called us about?" The first man in the room had a big grin as if he was seeing a family member after years apart, and addressed Shaun O'Brien like a brother.

"Hello Gil, I appreciate the company's help after all of this time, and on such short notice. No, I didn't get bored; I came down here and took over a small ministry, as funny a cover as that may seem. That guy on the bed is a rogue FBI operative that is down here to inflict hurt on one of my parishioners, and I just cannot abide with that," O'Brien replied.

"I understand everything except you being a pastor, and am glad to help, Shaun. We've got a team in place to take care of the other four operatives. These men are all mercs, and some very nasty individuals, or at least were some nasty individuals. I take it that you didn't use the same stuff on them that you did on our friend over there," Gil answered with a more serious tone.

"I used drain cleaner on them," O'Brien replied with an equally, and more deadly, serious tone in his voice, "They are just a disposal problem. This one is going to require some transportation back to Washington, and the special touch for which you are known. Let's go over the plan."

The men talked until about three o'clock before O'Brien was satisfied that they were all on the same page.

"I've got two more that have to be taken care of before dawn," He said in ending the meeting, "These are Federales on the DOJ payroll. It will be better if you all are gone with that package beforehand," He finished with a nod of his head in Kensey's direction.

Gil and his partner moved toward the bed to deal with Kensey who was having the most troubling of dreams. Gil turned back toward O'Brien as he was going out the door.

"Shaun, let's get together the next time you get to Washington. I'd like to catch up, and I know the Director would like to see you again. He sends his best, by the way."

"Thanks, Gil; tell the old man that I owe him," O'Brien stepped through the door and quietly disappeared.

As Special Agent Douglas Kensey slowly opened his eyes to the sight of his very unfamiliar surroundings, he felt disoriented at first, and then confused by the fact that his room was no longer cantaloupe orange, but the stark white of a hospital room. He slowly became aware of the IV drip in his arm, and the oxygen tube attached to his nose. In his initial panic, Kensey tried to sit up, only to find that he was also restrained to the bed rails, and a burly male nurse pushed him not so gently back into a flat position.

"You need to relax sir while I get the doctor. We've been waiting for you to wake up," he said before starting for the door.

"Nurse, what happened to me? Was I in an accident?" Kensey managed to ask through the fog in his head.

"No accident, I'm afraid. You've been shot several times," with that, the big man walked out of the room leaving Kensey to his imagination for only a very short time before three men in suits walked into the room.

"Agent Douglas Kensey?" one of the men asked while looking at the medical chart that was hanging at the foot of the bed.

"Yes, I'm *Special* Agent Kensey. Who are you, and where am I?" Kensey answered in as authoritarian a voice as he could muster in his extremely weakened and befuddled condition.

"*Agent* Kensey, you are in Walter Reed suffering from three gunshot wounds that you got while on an unauthorized trip to La Ceipas. Mr. Smith over here," indicating the man directly to his left, "is from the FBI and Mr. Gonzalez," indicating the man slightly behind and to his right, "is the ambassador from Honduras. I am Deputy Attorney General Paul Kruger, and we are very interested in this escapade of yours that has left four of our men and two Honduran Federal agents dead. What were you doing in Honduras, Agent Kensey, and who authorized this mission?"

Kensey felt trapped. He knew that somehow his simple mission to draw Bob Pike back to Honduran soil and away from Michael Tucker had gotten derailed, along with his career. Try as he might, there was no excuse that his drug soaked brain could invent that would help him now.

Anthony Morris had just arrived at the Florence, South Carolina office when his phone rang.

"Agent Morris here," He answered when he saw that the call was from a blocked number.

"Special Agent Morris, this is Deputy Director John Claiborne. I am cutting through the red tape involved to tell you personally that you have been reinstated to Special Agent in Charge, and are to take over the operation in Myrtle Beach, effective immediately! Do you understand?" Director Claiborne spoke with practiced authority.

Re-instated Special Agent in Charge Morris was taken aback at the announcement and was somewhat in shock as he replied, "Yes sir, I understand completely. Might I ask what has happened to Douglas Kensey?"

"Not at this time, although we will make an announcement in a couple of days after he has been debriefed fully. I especially want this situation with Michael Tucker and his family defused. Am I clear on that? I want any loose ends wrapped up, and this mess to go away, and that means pulling your undercover agent off his protection detail immediately. You didn't think that we wouldn't notice that did you, Morris?" the Director concluded.

"I thought that my actions to protect Officer Tucker were warranted, sir. I'll get Agent Biggs quietly transferred out of that area ASAP," Morris responded.

"Very good, Morris, contact me as soon as you have taken over the office down there," With that, the Director hung up leaving Special Agent Anthony Morris more than a little confused, but somewhat relieved now that it looked like the pressure was off Harry Albright and his family.

He exited the car and went into the building to pack the few items on the desk in the small office that he had taken over after the plot to kill Michael Tucker and his immediate family came into the light on national news.

The sound of the pack running in the swamp bottom came to the female's ears as she made her way slowly up the Little Pee Dee river basin, stopping frequently to test the wind. The loss of her kitten was still haunting her, and the pack cry of the coywolves struck a chord that caused rage to well up within her. The urge to kill overpowered her normal reticence to engage multiple coyotes and the big cat moved to intercept the pack with smooth, ground eating bounds.

The Alpha male ran with the scent of a frightened doe deer in his nostrils, and the diminished remnant of the pack followed closely behind. The doe stopped in a thick patch of undergrowth and raised her head to listen to the sound of her pursuers. As she turned to run deeper into the swamp and closer to the edge of the river, she was knocked off her feet by the one hundred and eighty-pound female, and quickly killed with a bite behind the head that separated her spinal cord. The cougar then effortlessly dragged the deer to a large oak with low-lying limbs and easily jumped the first limb ten feet up with the deer in her mouth. After caching her kill high up in the crotch of the live oak, she returned to the largest lower limb. Stretching full length on it as she awaited the approaching pack, the lioness seemed almost asleep, and in the darkness of the night, almost invisible to anything running below.

As the Alpha male ran with his nose pressed to the trail of the deer that would soon be the victim of the coy-wolf pack, he crossed the blood-soaked, scent flooded patch of ground where the lioness had made her kill, and stopped directly below the now crouching killer. His last conscious thought was the crunching sound the big cat's teeth made as they crushed through his skull at the back of his head.

The first two young males were on the scene in seconds. Startled and confused by the unexpected apparition in their path, they hesitated for the fraction of a second that it took for the cougar to rip the throat from the first, and then disembowel the second by grabbing him with her teeth about the throat while hooking the first claw of her right rear foot into the soft skin of his underbelly and pushing down savagely. His screams of terror alerted the last of the pack, stopping them from rushing headlong into the bloody chaos that was ensuing in the darkness of the swamp just a few feet away. Bereft of their leader, the pack dissolved into the night before the big cat could kill again, but they had lost the Alpha male and the dominant female in one day, effectively breaking all of the bonds that had held them together.

The cougar, her blood lust slaked, climbed back to the deer in the high part of the big oak, and began to eat her fill for the first time in many days. Tomorrow she would travel northward up the Pee Dee River bottom, but tonight she would satiate her hunger and the need for sleep.

CHAPTER 24

George Withers had a problem. Buried deep in his left leg were five number four aught buckshot pellets from Tuck's shotgun, and the wounds were festering. He had driven all of the way to Murrells Inlet to the CVS pharmacy to pick up cotton-tipped swabs and iodine, gauze and tape, but he could not acquire the one thing that was most needed, a prescription painkiller. Now he sat in the old motel that passed as a tourist hot spot in the summer, nursing a half finished bottle of cheap whiskey while he cleaned out the holes in his leg. The television volume was turned up to mask his moans as he dipped one after another of the long stick, iodine soaked surgical swabs into various bullet holes in his flesh.

He would dress his leg, and then try to find another car to replace the one that Hanna had shot the windows out of. Somehow, George's timing had gotten off. To be seen first, and then shot was something that happened to the less professional assassins that he knew and not something that happened to him. At least he had killed that damned dog.

George pulled his pants back on, grabbed his bag, and limped to the car. In just a few short minutes, there would be another ride under him, and another plan in his head to kill Hanna Albright Tucker. Unnoticed to George, the motel had installed a wireless security camera above the office, and it was recording his departure from the room, a small detail that he would not have overlooked just a few days before.

"Michael, are you asleep?" Hanna asked softly while resting her chin on Tuck's shoulder.

"No, well not now anyway, Hon. What's up?" Tuck responded with a smile as he rolled over to face his wife.

"I just wanted to talk. I'm really kind of afraid to go back to our house, but I know that we can't stay here indefinitely. Do you understand?" Hanna spoke softly with tears in her eyes. She knew what she was getting ready to ask her husband to do for her, and that scared her as much as the thought of George Withers finding her again.

"I've been giving it a lot of thought today, my Love, and I'm starting to believe that I need to get us away from here so that you and the baby and I can start over. Is that what you are feeling, too?" Tuck answered.

"Well, yes, sort of," Hanna answered, "but this killer needs to be caught if we are ever going to have some peace of mind no matter where we end up."

"Two killers, Hanna; I've got to kill that female cat before she kills another human. It would be hard for me to sleep at night knowing that we had let her go," Tuck had an edge to his voice, "George Withers will be caught; there are a lot of good people working on this, so it is just a matter of time. Now go to sleep, I've got a long day tomorrow," Tuck gave Hanna a big hug and a kiss before turning back over and drifting off into a troubled sleep.

Hanna snuggled his back and let her mind wander until sleep came almost an hour later. The one main thought was that they shouldn't have gotten rid of the houseboat.

Tuck eased out of bed at four thirty am without waking Hanna. Today was going to be extremely hectic, and he was meeting Bob and Harry for breakfast at Akel's Pancake House to start it off. Tuck knew that he could not prolong the confrontation with Joel Biggs indefinitely, so he had that in mind for the second thing to do. Colonel McCreery would know that Biggs was an FBI plant, of course, so in Tuck's mind that made him the enemy also, at least until events might prove otherwise. It was growing more and more apparent to Tuck that his career with the SCDNR was going to be short-lived. He just hoped that some of the loose ends would get wrapped up before he decided to quit.

The parking lot of Akel's was almost empty except for Bob's rental and one other official looking SUV that was parked on the other side of the building from it. Tuck opened the door to the characteristic smell of pancakes and disinfectant that always permeated the place in the early morning hours. Soon the tourists would start dragging in along with a few of the locals that still gathered here, but for now, it looked as though they would have the restaurant to themselves.

Tuck smiled at the hostess, an elderly Greek woman, and walked through to the side dining room where Bob and Harry were seated at a table close to the kitchen with Special Agent Anthony Morris.

"Hey, Tuck!" Bob called out a good-natured greeting, "We've just ordered coffee, and were waiting for you to get here."

Harry gave Tuck a big smile just before Morris said, "Good morning officer Tucker. I wanted to meet with all of you this morning to let you know that I am back in Myrtle Beach as Special Agent in Charge of our office here. That means taking control of the search for George Withers, and Harry," nodding in Harry Albright's direction, "tells me that you have some very good information about him."

Tuck hesitated for a moment and was saved from answering immediately by the arrival of the waitress for their orders.

"I'll have a stack of buttermilk pancakes with link sausage," he spoke first to her. The others placed their orders, and then Special Agent Morris looked at Tuck expectantly.

"We do have some documents on George Withers, but you have the same information, after all, he is working for you guys, isn't he?" Tuck answered Morris' question with a question, "My concern is for my wife. Can you promise me that she will be protected, Agent Morris?"

Morris' response was cut off by his cell phone ringing.

"Excuse me, gentlemen, this is an official call," And with that, he left the table and strode to the other end of the room.

"Why is he here this morning, Harry?" Tuck asked in a hushed voice, leaning in toward his father-in-law.

"Relax Tuck, Special Agent Morris is on our side, and always has been," Harry replied as Morris walked back to the table.

"Well, good news to report. Withers was spotted in Murrells Inlet last night, and we have people going over the room where he stayed as we speak. I've got to go down there and light a fire under my agents. We are getting close to this guy, and he is making mistakes that will get him caught. I'll call you, Harry, as soon as we have some more information. Tuck, I've also got people watching Hanna, and Joel Biggs has been pulled from his assignment as of last night," Morris finished and started for the door.

"Excuse me Agent Morris, but just what was his assignment, if I might ask?" Tuck queried the Special Agent.

"I had him protecting you, Officer Tucker," Morris answered with a smile over his shoulder without breaking stride.

"Well, I'll be..." Bob said in amazement, "It looks like we owe old Joel an apology, Tuck. He was one of the good guys after all."

"It is getting harder and harder to tell, that's for certain," Harry interjected.

Tuck just stared at the retreating back of Special Agent Anthony Morris for a few seconds, and then turned back to the table, "I hate to say it, but I am glad that Agent Morris is back on this case. That Kensey fellow didn't exactly inspire confidence, did he?"

"No, he certainly didn't," Harry answered, "I wonder what in the world happened to him?"

Bob just smiled a knowing smile and poured syrup on the pancakes that were set before them, "Harry, do you remember Shaun O'Brien, the salvage diver from Georgetown?"

"I know Shaun quite well, Bob, although it has been about two years since we last talked. I remember stories about Delta Force, CIA, and other covert activities, but we always just shrugged them off as rumors. Why do you ask?" Harry replied.

Before Bob could answer, Tuck interjected, "Shaun O'Brien… is he related to Margaret O'Brien, the reporter?"

"Yep, that is Maggie's father, but she hasn't seen much of him in the years since the divorce. Those 'rumors' about his clandestine activities hold a lot of truth, and he is the reason that Agent Kensey is not working the Myrtle Beach office. From what has been reported to me, Kensey went to LaCeiba the other night to harass Abigail in an effort to lure me away from here but apparently ran into a bunch of trouble down there. As a matter of fact, I would guess that his career with the feds is just about over," Bob told the story with a big smile.

"And this whole time we were worried about Abigail being down there by herself. Are you going to be able to get your scheduled meetings in before you return to Honduras, Bob?" Tuck asked, but before Bob could reply, Tuck's cell phone rang.

"Hi Ike, wait…slow down… what? Holy Crap! I'm on the way!" Tuck pushed himself back from the table and started for the door at a run.

"Tuck, what is it?" both Harry and Bob called to him simultaneously.

"A big bear has attacked a kid over in Carolina Forest a few minutes ago," Tuck yelled back over his shoulder without breaking stride.

"I'm coming with you!" Bob yelled, and then tossing the keys to Harry, "Harry if you'll settle up, here are the keys to the rental. I'll pick it up later."

"Go ahead, Bob. That boy isn't going to wait long," Harry replied as Bob ran for the door.

Tuck was already starting to back the big Ford out of the parking place when Bob jumped into the cab.

"Buckle up, Bob!" Tuck exclaimed as he wheeled the truck out onto Kings Highway with the lights flashing and smoke rolling off the inside rear tire. He hung a right on 62nd street, and raced to the bypass and then to Highway 501 at seventy plus miles an hour.

"I told those biologists last year that feeding the bears over on Lewiston was going to cause a conflict someday. They don't listen very well, do they?" Bob said to Tuck without expecting a reply. He and Tuck had discussed this very scenario many times over the past two years, and now they were living it.

The radio in the truck was spewing information from other law enforcement personnel already en-route to the scene of the attack.

Tuck keyed the mike and called Junior Knowles, "Private Knowles come in."

"Private Knowles here, Lieutenant, I'm already rolling. Have you seen Private Biggs today? I can't raise him," Knowles answered almost immediately.

"Private Biggs is working another case so we are on our own for now. Meet me at the entrance to Carolina Forest, and we will go in together...Tucker out," Tuck replied.

"Roger that Lieutenant, I'll be there in a few minutes...Knowles out," Junior finished the call

"That area off Carolina Farms Boulevard is pretty remote, Bob. I'm betting that bear is the same one that has been raiding the garbage cans out there. What do you think?" Tuck asked as they crossed the Waccamaw river bridge.

"If it is, he is about four hundred pounds. This could be a problem, Tuck. That area is mostly thick pine cover behind those cookie cutter houses. Where did the attack take place?" Bob replied.

"Almost at the end of Carolina Farms Blvd, the kid was waiting on the early school bus," Tuck replied, "When we get there, how about pulling the rifle and shotgun from the back while I find out just what happened."

Junior Knowles was waiting for them as they turned onto Carolina Forest Blvd so Tuck just waved him to drop in behind and follow then out. Just ahead was an ambulance with lights and siren screaming, and coming up from behind at a high rate of speed was a black SUV that looked suspiciously like a government vehicle. It fell in behind Knowles and followed them the several miles to the scene.

As they reached their destination, Tuck counted at least a dozen official cars and the WLIB news van of Maggie O'Brien. It was obvious that she was going to be on them as soon as they stopped, so Bob volunteered to run point.

"I'll keep Maggie occupied while you get all of the particulars, Tuck. We need to work fast if that bear has taken the child away from this area as all of that chatter seems to indicate."

Tuck's mind was working overtime even before he brought the truck to a stop where Ike was waving them in. As he got out, Bob shouted to the red-haired reporter and motioned her over to his side of the truck. Tuck looked back to see Joel Biggs coming up behind Knowles dressed in civilian clothes.

"I'm here to help, Lieutenant. We can talk later if you like," Joel said before Tuck could get a word out.

"Very well, Joel. Can you take Private Knowles and start tracking this animal while I take a look at the scene? Bob has my shotgun, you might need it," Tuck responded quickly and efficiently. It was necessary to track and kill this animal quickly before the trail washed out from the forecasted rain.

"I'm on it Lieutenant, but I brought my own weapons this time," Agent Joel Biggs replied, and then to Knowles, "You need to go get your shotgun just in case we run this thing down."

Tuck met Ike in the front yard of the new home in this new subdivision. The houses were all two story middle-class homes that looked like they had been built from one set of plans. Ike led the way around back.

"This is pretty gruesome, Tuck. Apparently, that bear grabbed the girl just as she took a bag of trash to the trashcan before going around the front to catch the school bus. From the amount of blood at the scene, I don't think this is going to end well," Ike filled Tuck in on the details of the attack somberly.

The back yard was filled with law enforcement personnel and the EMT crew. There were onlookers from the neighborhood also peering nervously from the confined area where the first responders had set up a perimeter. Tuck followed Ike directly to the trashcans where the attack occurred.

"This is a big bear, Ike. I'm guessing around four to five hundred pounds from that paw print and these claw marks. From the blood trail, he struck off about north-northwest toward the substation. Can you get some men over there to try and block off that area? We will start tracking from here," Tuck quickly evaluated the situation and came up with a plan.

"Sure thing Tuck! I'll call right now," Ike replied as he keyed his shoulder mike and put in the call for more manpower.

Bob came up behind them with several more deputies and two troopers.

"Where do you want us, Tuck?" he asked.

"Bob, you will take Private Knowles, and fan these men out in a line stretching back toward that cul-de-sac. Joel and I will track this bear. Borrow Knowles's shotgun and stay close to me on this end," Tuck explained the plan to Bob as he took his .308 Remington 700 tactical and racked a 168 grain round into the chamber. Joel was already checking the area around the attack with a new UTAS UT-15 shotgun loaded with six, three-inch magnum, number four aught buck in the right magazine tube, and six, three-inch magnum, rifled slugs in the left magazine tube and equipped with a seven and a half inch barrel extension.

"Nice weapon, Joel!" Tuck said while eying the short and deadly shotgun that Biggs was carrying. Well, let's find him and pray that he hasn't killed that kid yet…or worse," Tuck finished quietly as he and Joel started a fast paced, but quiet walk along the obvious trail.

The big-bodied bear had covered almost half of the three-quarter mile distance to the substation feeder road when he stopped to examine his prize. The screams that had a first infuriated him were now just an occasional moan as the little girl's blood loss from the teeth marks in her right shoulder caused her to mercifully drift in and out of consciousness.

He wasn't really hungry since the DNA sample pen was always full of corn, but his natural instinct had taken over when this small human had trespassed on his turf while he was raiding the garbage. Now he watched her for about two minutes and then rolled her over with a swat of his large paw. A small moan escaped her lips as the ribs that had been broken in the initial attack shot sharp pains throughout her body, and the bear backed up slightly.

A slight breeze carried in the faint sounds of the humans in the woods, still several hundred yards away, and the black bear stood on his hind legs to better smell the approach of his adversaries. Dropping back on all fours, he decided to take his prize with him and grabbed the girl's leg in his teeth. Her scream of pain startled him, causing the bear to drop her and back off several feet. It was then that he heard Tuck shout, "Carla, Carla Templeton!"

The bear turned toward the sound and grunted while smacking his mouth making a popping sound.

The first 168 grain round of Tuck's Remington 700 caught the bear right of the center of the chest with a loud smack but missed the heart. The bear rolled over at the impact and tried to run off into the deeper woods, but was met with two blasts from the UT-15; one a withering charge of four aught buckshot, and the other a five hundred grain rifled slug which entered behind his left shoulder shattering ribs and tissue while tearing its way into his heart.

Tuck had risked a shot through almost forty yards of thick pine at his first sight of the bear, but Joel had been ahead of Tuck to his left; thirty yards closer to Carla when Tuck fired, which brought the wounded animal within a few yards of the deadly fire of the UTAS UT-15 as it tried to escape.

"Is she alive, Tuck?" Joel called out as he ran to where Tuck was bent over the little girl.

"Just barely, Ike will be here in a second with the medics. Is that bear dead?" Tuck asked as he raised her head slightly to put his jacket under her for a pillow while keeping pressure on the worst of the punctures in her thin shoulder and Joel just nodded in the affirmative.

Then Tuck said to the frightened child, "It's all right now, Carla. You just hold on for a few more minutes, and we will get you out of here."

Carla just looked up at his face for a brief second before her eyes closed in unconsciousness again, but Tuck thought that he had seen a small smile bend the corners of her mouth.

The woods was suddenly filled with rescuers so Tuck handed Carla over to the EMTs, and turned his attention to the bear that now lay dead a few yards away.

Turning to Bob Pike and Junior Knowles who had run up out of breath, Tuck said, "Private Knowles, the biologists will be here shortly to do a post-mortem on that animal. I want you to stay with him until they get here, and then give me a call after they've picked him up. Not a word to the reporters either, understood?"

"Yes sir, Lieutenant. I understand," Knowles responded as Tuck, Bob, and Joel walked away from the circus-like scene.

"Well Bob, kind of like old times, isn't it?" Tuck asked jokingly.

"Too much so, I'm afraid. I'm going to get back on my schedule after this so I can enjoy my retirement. Thank God, that little girl is still alive. That in itself is something of a miracle," Bob replied.

"What about you Joel?" Tuck asked, "Are you going back to being an agent again?"

Joel looked at them both and grinned. "I can absolutely say that anything that Special Agent Morris has me doing will pale in comparison to taking care of you two."

With that, he shook both men's hands and walked back to his SUV.

Just as he was about to get in the Ford DNR truck, Tuck was interrupted by Maggie O'Brien, "Lieutenant Tucker, can I have a minute of your time please?"

Tuck turned toward the reporter and her cameraman with his best public servant face forward and asked, "What can I do for you, Maggie?"

"Can you give me an official statement on the bear attack for our viewing audience Lieutenant? Were you surprised to find Carla Templeton alive?" Maggie asked.

"I really don't want to comment on the attack until after all of the tests are run on that bear. These types of occurrences are extremely rare, and I certainly would like to tell your viewers that there is no danger of another attack happening anytime soon. However, everyone should be aware that bears, cougars, poisonous snakes, alligators, feral hogs, and coyotes do exist in this area, so reasonable caution is prudent. Now I really have to get on with other business Maggie," With that, Tuck got into the truck and shut the door.

"I see that your strong suit is never going to be diplomacy, Tuck."

Tuck just looked at his friend and ex-partner with a grimace as he dialed the Colonel's number, "Good morning Colonel

McNeery. We had another animal attack this morning, this time, a bear grabbed a child in the Carolina Forest area. No, she survived, although she has been badly bitten. Yes, sir, that is the area that Bob Pike warned us about, and probably the same bear, but DNA evidence will prove or disprove that. Yes, sir, I'll have a report to you in about an hour. No sir, I didn't make any statements to the press. Well, of course, I talked to the reporter, but it is difficult to avoid them in a situation like this. Yes, sir, it won't happen again," Tuck hung up the phone with a disgusted look on his face.

Bob remarked with a laugh, "I'm sure glad I'm retired"

"Bob, I'm thinking of quitting the DNR," Tuck spoke bluntly, "Hanna is worn out from what has happened this last few months, and I am kind of fed up with not only having to deal with an absurd amount of animal attacks but also having to look over my shoulder all of the time because the government has me in their sights. I want to take care of Hanna, so we are going to leave as soon as we can find a buyer for the house."

"Well, I can't say that your decision is unexpected, just look at all that you two have been up against since you got married. I've got a great idea, why don't you come to Honduras with Abigail and me until after the baby is born?" Bob offered.

"We'll pray about it, Bob. Hanna and I were thinking about getting another boat and spending some time on it. Maybe Honduras would be a great trip for us. We'll see. I'll run you back to Harry's and drop you off, and then I've got to handle a complaint over at the Bucksport Marina this morning before noon. It's going to be a very long day," Tuck concluded.

Bob just gave him a big smile before calling Harry.

CHAPTER 25

Tuck dropped off Bob at Harry's and then spent a few minutes with Hanna before making the drive to the Bucksport Marina. As he pulled up to the Marina store and restaurant, his eyes ventured to the dock where the 'Michael's Home' had been berthed for the last two years. To his surprise, the slip was filled with the graceful lines of a forty-two foot West Sail, a strange sight in this small marina. Tuck gave it little thought except to think of how nice it would be if he and Hanna could just get on board and sail away from all of their anxieties, which seemed to be magnified day by day.

As he walked into the store the harbormaster called to him, "Hello Lieutenant Tucker, we certainly have missed having you around since you sold the houseboat."

"Hello George, what was the problem that you wanted to see me about?" Tuck liked George Tomlinson, the harbormaster of this marina, but right now, he was more interested in handling whatever was going on and then getting back to his office to write the report that the Colonel was waiting on.

"Well Lieutenant, last night someone killed a small alligator in the river for its tail. The carcass washed up between that West Sail and the dock this morning, causing a bit of commotion among our guests. I wanted to report it to you personally because I knew that you would handle the situation," was the reply, "The owner is waiting on board to talk to you about it."

Tuck got the distinct impression that something was amiss with the alligator scenario, but decided that it wouldn't hurt to talk to the vessel's owner, "All right George, I'll go over and talk to the man. What is his name?"

"Albert Jordan, Lieutenant. Just tell him that I sent you over. I like for my guests to feel that I've got their best interests firmly in hand if you know what I mean," George responded with just a little too much enthusiasm.

As Tuck walked back across the parking lot to the slip where the West Sail was docked, he couldn't help but admire her sleek lines and the enclosed cabin. He knew from listening to his Dad that these boats were state of the art vessels, but had been discontinued in the late seventies for a variety of reasons. For a boat that was about forty years old, this old girl had been given loving care.

"Ahoy, the 'Betty Anne'," Tuck called as he approached the boat from the stern and noticed her name.

"Hello there, you must be Lieutenant Tucker, I've been expecting you," a very warm sounding voice sounded from inside of the cabin, followed by an older gentleman's head popping out of the cabin aft curtain.

"Come aboard, come aboard," The old man motioned Tuck to the rail.

Tuck stepped lightly onto the deck and shook Albert's hand, "Mister Jordan, I understand that someone poached an alligator, and it washed up here between your boat and the dock," Tuck began his inquiry.

"Yes, the poor animal is right up by the bow. I've tied him off and saved the body for you to dispose of, but before you do, could I offer you a cup of coffee? It is fresh," Albert said in a very inviting voice, almost pleading, "Please join me for a few minutes, I don't often have guests."

Tuck hesitated for just a couple of seconds and then said, "I would like a cup of coffee sir. It's been a very rough morning, and I didn't get to finish my first cup."

The stinking carcass of the bloated 'gator could wait a few minutes longer as could the paperwork because Tuck really wanted to see the inside of this beautiful boat.

"We will take our coffee in the aft cabin, Officer Tucker," Albert said as he motioned Tuck to sit in a small deck chair that sat in one corner of the enclosed cockpit, "I'll go below decks and bring it right up."

Tuck ran his hands over the teak trim of the cockpit and admired the brass trim of the binnacle. He squatted to look below deck and saw the well-maintained galley and the space forward.

Albert came back up the hatch with a coffee service for two and a plate of cookies beside the silver pot on the serving tray.

"It wouldn't be a proper coffee break without the cookies, now would it Lieutenant Tucker," His cheery voice seemed like a light coming from the companionway.

Tuck reached down to take the tray and set it on the small table that sat between the two chairs. He then waited for Albert to sit himself down before reaching over to pour the old man's coffee, and then one for himself. As they engaged in small talk about the boat, and Albert's adventures on it, the talk turned to Albert's recently deceased wife, Betty Anne, his lifelong companion and his best friend who had succumbed to cancer just a few months ago while the couple was in the Bahamas. Albert had no family left and no desire to continue sailing without Betty Anne at his side as he explained to Tuck. Something is his story reminded Tuck of how close he came to losing Hanna just a few short months ago, and he understood how hard this must be Albert.

As Albert wound down his story, Tuck asked, "What are you going to do now, Mr. Jordan?"

"Please call me Albert, Lieutenant Tucker. We're old friends now, I think," He said with a big smile and poured another cup for Tuck.

"Okay then, Albert. I used to live here on my houseboat before I married my wife. We tried it for a short while afterward, but getting a house seemed to make more sense to us then. Now, I'm not so certain that we made the right choice," Tuck opened up to

Albert as if he was talking to his grandfather, whom he had never met.

"I don't believe in coincidence, Lieutenant Tucker. I made up my mind that it was time to sell the 'Betty Anne' and find myself a little house in this area. I want to bring my Betty Anne home where we can visit in the afternoons. It is a long way to the Bahamas where she was interred."

Tuck knew that what he wanted to ask was a long shot at best, but Harry had taught him to not believe in coincidence, but rather divine providence, "Albert, I have a nice home that we want to sell, and you have a beautiful sailboat that you want to sell, would you possibly be interested in a trade?"

Albert swirled the coffee in his cup for a moment and looked as if he were lost in thought, then he looked up at Tuck with a big grin and said, "Possibly, Lieutenant Tucker, quite possibly."

Tuck felt as if a big weight had been lifted from his shoulders as he stood up to leave, "Thank you for your hospitality Albert. I would like you to meet my wife, Hanna. Maybe we could have dinner at our place and talk about this some more. How does that sound?"

"I would like that very much. Bring your wife over tomorrow so she can meet 'Betty Anne' and we will set something up. Now go get that stinking alligator off my dock!" Albert said with a big grin before returning to the galley area with the coffee service.

Tuck walked down the dock and untied the small alligator from the cleat that it was secured to. After dragging it onto the dock and across the parking lot, Tuck retrieved a tarp from the truck bed and wrapped the alligator carcass before loading it into the truck bed. Tuck finished up and then walked back over to the marina to wash his hands. As he came through the door, he saw George standing with his back toward him, talking on the phone.

"I'm excited, too, Hanna," George was saying, "He's over there right now talking to Albert. I'll let you know as soon as we do."

"Let her know what, exactly," Tuck demanded.

"Oh, Lieutenant Tucker, I didn't hear you come in," George answered with a flustered tone in his voice.

"Let her know what?" Tuck repeated the question sternly.

"Well, Hanna was talking to my wife Chloe the other day, and she mentioned that with everything that has happened, she wished that she could trade the house back in on the houseboat again. I knew that Albert was looking for a house so I kind of, well sort of, set up a meeting," George answered nervously.

"Did you kill that alligator, George?" Tuck asked without breaking eye contact.

"No sir, I did not!" George was emphatic in his answer, "I found that in the river this morning and decided to use it to get you over here."

"Well, I suppose your ruse worked well enough, George, but please let me be the one to tell Hanna that we are not going to trade the house for the boat. That is something that needs to be worked out between a husband and wife," Tuck then turned and walked to the door.

"Absolutely, Lieutenant Tucker, I won't get involved again, I promise," George was sucking up in a big way to Tuck's back, and couldn't see the big smile on Tuck's face as he walked back to the truck with his hands smelling like dead fish.

CHAPTER 26

The high water levels of an early spring kept the big cat closer to the habitation of humans than she liked, but it also meant that the chance of finding a fat dog or cat was also better the further away from the river that she traveled.

She had crossed Highway 378 early that morning, and was now hungry and tired. As luck would have it, the yapping of a dog close by signaled the end of her hunger, so she immediately moved quietly in the direction of the noise.

Outside of an old house trailer, a large pit bull dog was chained to his doghouse, and a mixed breed dog stood barking at the back door of the trailer to be let in. Moving ever so slowly with her body pressed to the ground, the big female stalked her prey through the tangle of briars and trash that littered the back yard of the property, soon coming within twenty feet of the pit bull without being seen.

Suddenly the back door of the trailer flew open and a haggard looking man screamed at the dog, "Shut up you worthless mutt!" followed by a brick being thrown that narrowly missed the animal as he fled with his tail between his legs. The brick hit the top of the doghouse causing the big bulldog to jump to his feet and swing to face his possible attacker. The cougar was waiting for the opportunity. With incredible speed, she covered the few feet between her and the pit bull and launched herself onto his back while sinking her teeth into the back of his head. The dog gave a scream of pain and then managed to grasp the cougar's left paw between his powerful jaws. The sound of bones breaking and the excruciating pain in her mangled paw brought a scream from the cat's mouth, causing her to momentarily relax her grip on the bulldog.

The dog shook off his pain and surprise to viciously attack the cat head on, trying to get to her throat, but the cougar was faster and managed to leap away from the attack as the door to the trailer flew open again to reveal the unkempt man pointing a Taurus snub nose .38 Special in the direction of the cat. Unfortunately, the first shot not only hit the bulldog, but also, the muzzle flash ignited the highly volatile fumes of acetone, red phosphorus, and petroleum ether that were given off as a byproduct of his methamphetamine production. That generated a fireball that instantly reduced the trailer to a pile of twisted, burning rubble, and blew the man's burned body directly out into the back yard over twenty yards from where the back stoop had been moments before.

Dazed by the explosion and in pain from the savage bite of the pit bull dog, the cat limped back toward the wooded area behind the trailer that she had come from. As she slowly covered the distance to the woods, she found the burned man lying in a state of shock. Even though she was disoriented from the force of the blast, the cougar still recognized her need to eat, and this was an easy kill to make.

The sound of sirens in the distance did little to muffle the screams of the victim, as the cat's sharp claws opened his abdomen in a search for the organ meat that all cats love.

"Hey George, look over here!" the first volunteer to reach the back of the house called to one of the sheriff's deputies that was on the scene of the meth lab explosion, "That dog looks like he was in a fight, and there is a bullet hole in his side also."

As the two men looked at the wounded animal, the deputy made a call to the local animal rescue shelter. His call was interrupted by the other man's excited shouting, "Look over there!" followed by a hand pointing in the direction that he meant.

Sticking up above the brush and trash about twenty yards away was the unmistakable, twitching tail of the big cougar!

The deputy pulled his nine millimeter Glock 31 and fired three quick rounds where he thought the cat's body should be which resulted in the cat bounding off into the woods at a furious pace.

With the deputy calling for backup on his radio, the two men hurried to the spot where that cat had been seconds before. There on the ground in front of them was the badly burned and eviscerated body of Virgil Socks.

"Holy crap!" was all the deputy could get out as his partner spun quickly to avoid puking on the corpse.

It was evident from the frozen mask of terror on his charred face that Virgil had been alive when the feeding started.

The first shot from the deputy's Glock had hit the ground directly under the feeding cat, which, because of her hunger and the shock of the explosion, had been oblivious to the presence of the two men. As she jumped away from the body of her victim, the second shot plowed into her right hip just below the tail and exited three inches forward, leaving a clean wound that burned like fire. The third shot missed, and the cat wasted no time in getting to the woods and the relative safety that it offered. She had not finished feeding, but now her survival instincts were in overdrive as she hobbled on three legs trying to put distance between herself and her tormentors.

Distracted by the pain in her crushed paw and hindquarter, the cougar ran back to the sanctuary of the swamp bottom that had been her home for the past few years. As she bounded up the embankment of Highway 378, she made the leap across the westbound lanes in two strides, but her broken paw crumpled under her as she landed on the eastbound side of the highway, causing her to stumble momentarily as she fought the pain and made an effort to regain her stride.

The Toyota 4Runner driven by Bob Littleford caught the cat mid-grill and threw her unceremoniously across the guardrail and into the brush below the embankment. Bob immediately slid to a halt and made a call to the Highway Patrol. In his seventy-six years of living in the Conway area, he had never seen a cougar. Bob was not about to get out of the vehicle until someone was there with a gun!

CHAPTER 27

In the weeks following the demise of the female cougar, Tuck and Hanna busied themselves with making the final preparations for transferring ownership of the house in Conway to Albert Jordan, and the ownership of the 'Betty Anne' to the Tuckers. This included having a large moving sale to reduce the amount of stowage that they would have to have aboard the West Wind, renting space for everything that wouldn't fit, and then making the run to McClellanville to haul the 'Betty Anne' and have her surveyed for the insurance company and the Coast Guard documentation.

Tuck and Hanna sat one evening on the aft deck and talked about a new name for the 'Betty Anne'.

"Michael, do you remember how we used to walk to the beach from Daddy's house and listen to the night wind as it made the surf roar?" Hanna asked.

"I remember that you used to like that time of the evening more than any other," Tuck answered while drawing Hanna a little closer, "Why?"

"I was just thinking that 'Night Wind' would be a good name for the boat," She replied.

They sat for a minute in silence just listening to the evening sounds of the waterway before Tuck replied, "I like it, 'Night Wind' has a certain ring to it."

"Oh, Michael, you're not just saying that to appease an old pregnant lady are you? Do you really like the name?" Hanna asked hopefully.

"Tomorrow I'll get the papers in order for a name change, Hanna. Maybe we can get Albert to take us on a shakedown cruise so I can get the feel of our new home before too much longer," He finished with a grin.

"I'd like that Michael, but when are you going to turn your resignation into the Colonel? They don't seem to appreciate all that you and Bob did for the DNR, so why drag it out?" Hanna was anxious to start a new chapter in their lives, and the tone of her voice let Tuck know that his procrastination needed to come to a screeching halt.

"Before the end of the week, I promise," Tuck responded with what seemed like misery in his voice.

While he didn't have much desire to stay with the DNR after all of the corruption and secrecy of the past year, he wasn't really ready for the change that leaving would bring, especially since his son was going to be born in a few short months.

"I wonder what we can do in Honduras to make some money?" He asked Hanna quietly.

"God will provide, Michael Tucker!" She said sternly, "He has certainly been good to us with all that we've been through, and I know that He has a plan for you and me, so quit worrying. Besides, Albert is giving us more than fifty thousand for the house in addition to the boat, we'll be fine."

Tuck gave her a big smile and leaned over to kiss her on the forehead, "Let's get to Harry's and get some real sleep tonight. You've been working way too hard for an 'old pregnant lady', and I have an early day tomorrow."

"Okay, Love. I'm kind of bushed anyway. You lock up and I'll get the truck," Hanna said as she moved to the gangway and down the dock to where Tuck had parked the DNR Ford. Tuck watched her walk away and thought how perfect this would be if his old mutt, Weston, were running alongside Hanna, eager to jump in the back of the truck. As he started to turn back to the business at hand, a glint of something shiny in the front of a late model Buick parked by the marina office caught his eye.

Quickly, Tuck picked up his three-cell flashlight and directed the beam into the front window of the Buick, which suddenly flew into motion with the front tires barking as it left the marina in a hurry.

Tuck ran to the truck to check on Hanna, but she had seen the actions of the Buick and gotten down behind the heavy pickup for shelter, just in case.

"We need to get out of here, now!" Tuck shouted as he ran to the truck.

Hanna jumped in the passenger seat as fast as her pronounced belly would let her as Tuck fired the Ford up.

"Who was that Michael?" she asked nervously.

"I'm not sure," he replied, "but I'm calling Ike to have them keep an eye on the boat tonight."

As George Withers roared out of the parking lot of the Bucksport Marina and turned right onto State Highway 26-28, he immediately realized that he had made another mistake that could result in his being arrested, if not shot. Highway 26-28 would bring him out on Highway 701, which is also where the local sheriff's deputies would be waiting to apprehend him. It was very careless of him to approach the Tuckers so closely in the early evening, and now that carelessness jeopardized his entire plan to kill Hanna Tucker.

George quickly decided to take the first left that he came to, which was Treatment Road. He roared down the road past the water treatment plant and then turned to the right at the first intersection onto a narrow dirt road that led in the general direction of Highway 701. Port Harrelson Road soon gave him the opportunity to turn back to the right, but that direction would lead back to the entrance to the Bucksport Marina, so he kept on driving straight across the main road, hoping that this dirt path would ultimately get him back to the main highway, and a chance of freedom.

As the road dwindled to a dirt lane, George Withers killed his lights, and then slowed to a crawl to survey his situation. Directly in front of his stolen Buick was a small house with several vehicles and a boat in the yard. George came to a stop, killed the engine, and got out of the car quietly.

It did not seem as if anyone detected his presence, so he left the car and worked his way through the pines to the house. Once on the small porch, he heard laughter coming from inside. It was obvious that someone had the television volume turned up high and at least one, possibly two people were watching something that they thought was funny. George's hand slipped into his jacket pocket and came out with the suppressed .22 caliber Mark II Ruger that was his favorite pistol for his type of work.

Quietly he made his way across the porch to the living room window and peered into the well-lit room. Two men sat with their backs to the window engrossed in the program that was on the TV and oblivious to George's presence. The little .22 popped softly two times and both men slumped in their seats. George quickly let himself in through the unlocked front door, and within a few short minutes found a set of keys to an older Chevy truck that was parked in the drive as if it had been the last to arrive.

He left the TV blaring and returned to his Buick to retrieve some supplies, and to wipe it down for any prints that he might have been careless enough to leave. When he had driven the Buick as far into the woods surrounding the house as he could, George returned to the old truck and drove it slowly through the sparse pines the remaining two hundred yards to Highway 701. Once there, he drove up the slight embankment, turned left towards Williamsburg County and away from Conway. Hanna Tucker's demise would have to wait for a more opportune time. Right now, he needed to find a place to hide and redress his leg wound that was festering.

CHAPTER 28

Tuck was almost into Columbia to turn in his resignation when the call came from Ike Baumgarner, "Tuck, we found the two Jacobs brothers dead in their place about a mile from the marina. Both had been shot in the back of the head with a small caliber round. Just off hand, I would say that it's Withers again. Whoever did it took John Jacobs' truck and drove it through the woods to the highway."

"Okay Ike, I'm taking care of that business with the Colonel this morning. How about making certain that someone is watching Hanna until I get back?" Tuck tried to not sound as concerned as he felt.

"I've already worked it out with the Feds and Myrtle Beach to keep a sharp eye on the house, Tuck, but you need to get back as soon as possible. Hanna needs to be in a safe place, pronto!" Ike finished before ending the call.

"Just what we need today," Tuck thought darkly, "another attack by that deranged S.O.B."

He pulled the truck into the parking lot and went inside for his appointment with the Colonel who had not been told the nature of Tuck's business. Colonel McNeery had him ushered in immediately.

"Lieutenant Tucker, good morning. What is this all about?" the Colonel asked.

Tuck handed Colonel McNeery the envelope with his resignation papers inside after shaking his hand, "Colonel, I'm handing you my resignation, sir. My wife and I need a change of scenery, and I need to be in a location that will provide her with more security."

Colonel McNeery just stared at the envelope for a minute and then said, "I understand that you've been through a lot in the past few months, Tucker, but are you certain that you want to flush a promising career down the drain like this?"

"Yes sir, I am absolutely certain. Last night the maniac that tried to kill us at the house showed up at the marina. I scared him off, but he killed two men during his escape. Now I have to worry every minute about Hanna while we are anywhere near Myrtle Beach," Tuck responded, "In light of that, I need to make my notice as short as possible, and I hope you will understand, sir"

"I hate to see you go, son, but I would probably do the same in your shoes. If you will work on call for the next two weeks, I will shift some of our resources down there so you can leave," McNeery offered his hand in dismissal.

Tuck shook the hand that was offered and thanked the Colonel. He almost ran to the truck in his haste to get back to the beach and Hanna. They needed to leave for Honduras as soon as they could pack and wrap up the loose ends with the house. Bob Pike was ready to leave and would be a boon as an extra seasoned hand on the big sailboat that Tuck knew very little about.

As soon as he cleared the parking lot of the SCDNR headquarters, Tuck called Hanna.

"Hi Hon, Is everything all right there?" Tuck asked when she answered the phone.

"I'm good Michael, how did it go with the Colonel?" Hanna answered sweetly.

"Well, I think that he understood our situation, but he was none too happy with me, that was obvious," Tuck replied, "Listen, Hanna, I want you to stay real close to the house today. That was George Withers last night, and I don't feel comfortable with you driving around town without me."

"Oh, Tuck," She responded, "It's all over the news about those poor men that he killed last night. I hope they catch him soon, and I hope you hurry up and get your butt back home!"

"I'm on the way. Tell Bob that we need to make some concrete plans tonight. I love you," Tuck ended the call with his mind running at full speed. How could a psychopath like George Withers evade every law enforcement agency that had been hunting him for months unless someone in one of the top-level agencies did not want him found? They all knew by now that Withers was an FBI assassin, but what if they just assumed that he was a rogue agent? What if he actually was still working for the bureau or someone deeply embedded in that organization? Tuck knew that this had to be the only logical explanation, but whom could he talk to about it? Somehow, he had to protect Hanna and their unborn child, even if it cost everything that he had.

The drive back to Myrtle Beach was uneventful, which gave Tuck time to make some tentative plans regarding his fast approaching departure date. They had to finish the paperwork for the house sale, and the paperwork involved in buying the 'Betty Anne' and changing the name to 'Night Wind'. There was still the learning curve for sailing the vessel in open water, something that Tuck had only done with his father on the rare occasions that they sailed. Usually, they were running a sport fishing boat or poling a bateau in the swamp bottoms of the Pee Dee and Waccamaw Rivers.

There wouldn't be time for a shakedown with Albert now that George Withers was back and so intent on harming Hanna. They would have to rely on Bob Pike's expertise until Tuck could master the sailing art in deep water; something that he was certain would not take much time.

Tuck pulled into Harry's driveway and gave the horn a quick blast to signal his arrival. That brought Hanna out of the house with a big smile on her face and a wave of her hand. Tuck was so anxious to see Hanna, that he did not notice the late model Toyota pickup with a john boat and trailer hooked up that was sitting a half block down the street. Neither did he notice that the driver of the truck was the disgraced ex-Special Agent in Charge, Douglas Kensey, who was festering over the manner of his disgrace, which he laid directly at Tuck's door.

When Tuck and Hanna had gone inside, Kensey drove past the house slowly and out of the neighborhood.

"Where is everyone?" Tuck asked as soon as they were inside by themselves.

"Daddy, Kathryn, and Bob went down to the church to get the yard work done, and get ready for Wednesday night. They should be back in a couple of hours," Hanna replied.

"Well, I'm glad for the time alone, Hanna. We need to talk about this trip that we are going to take, and how it will affect Harry and Kathryn and your sisters when the baby is born," Tuck had taken her by the hand and led her into the living room so that they could talk.

"I've been thinking about this, Michael. This is Daddy's first grandchild, and he is going to be so disappointed if we are not around when the baby is born. Then again, if we stay, the baby might not be born," Hanna was close to tears.

Tuck drew her close and told her, "We can stay if you want, Honey, but Harry and Kathryn can also come to Honduras for a week or so. In fact, that was Harry's idea when we talked about this last week. I think that we should pray about this and see what Harry has to say when they get home."

They were interrupted by Tuck's cell phone ringing. He crossed the room to where it lay on the piano and picked it up. Before answering Tuck looked at the caller ID and spoke to Hanna, "It's Bob," "Hey Bob are you guys going to be long?"

"Tuck, where is Hanna?" Bob asked in a hushed tone.

"She's right here with me, why?" Tuck answered, immediately concerned.

"Harry has had a heart attack and is at Grand Strand Emergency. Kathryn and I are with him. Tuck it doesn't look good. You need to get Hanna up here very quickly," Bob answered; the strain in his voice was evident.

"We are on the way!" Tuck ended the call and then turned to Hanna, "Harry's in the hospital, Hanna. We've got to go now!"

Hanna threw her hand over her mouth and tears started streaming down her face, "Not Daddy, Tuck. Oh God, please take care of my Daddy!"

Tuck wrapped his arm around her shoulder and moved her toward the door and out to the truck. The trip to the hospital took about ten minutes, and Bob met them at the emergency room door.

"Hanna, Harry is in the back. Kathryn is with him. We need to hurry," Bob talked quickly as he took Hanna by the arm and led her and Tuck to the triage room.

Harry was on a ventilator when they walked in and Kathryn was standing by the bed, holding his hand. Tears were streaming down her face as she prayed over her husband. Hanna stepped up close and hugged her stepmother, and then leaned over and kissed Harry on the forehead.

"I love you, Daddy," she whispered weakly, "Please wake up and look at me."

Harry lay unresponsive, and the only sound in the room was from the monitor, which beeped every few seconds.

Bob took Tuck by the arm and led him outside the curtain that separated the room from the rest of the E.R., "Harry's gone, Tuck. They left him on the ventilator until Hanna could get here, but there is no brain activity," Bob was close to tears and he made the announcement to his friend.

"What happened, Bob? Harry was in perfect health," Tuck asked.

"It looks like a massive coronary. Harry was mowing outside the church by the road. A car came by and he raised his arm to wave at the guy, and then dropped like a stone to the ground. By the time that I got to him, he was gone. Kathryn called 911, but it was too late to help him," Bob related the events to Tuck, just as he saw them.

"What kind of car?" Tuck asked, his mind running scenarios in high gear.

"Some kind of a truck, I think a Toyota with a boat on the back," Bob answered.

"I'm going back in to be with Hanna. Can you call Special Agent Morris and get him down here? We need to talk," Tuck said to Bob as he turned to walk back into the room.

"Sure Tuck. I'll do it right now," Bob replied, leaving Harry's family to pay their final respects.

CHAPTER 29

"Lieutenant Tucker, I can swear to you that the FBI has not run any ongoing covert operations against you, the Pikes, or the Albrights since the Lawrence Richards debacle!" Special Agent Morris exclaimed in a hushed voice as he and Tuck stood outside of the emergency room, "Now I know that George Withers is off his chain, but this was not George. It doesn't match his M.O. Besides, we don't know if this wasn't a naturally occurring heart attack. Harry was under a lot of stress also; you have to admit."

"I've been around long enough to be suspicious when any government employee starts making excuses, especially when they are from the same agency as the psycho that is trying to kill my wife. All I'm asking for is for you to authorize an autopsy to look for anything out of the way that might have contributed to Harry's death. I did see a Toyota truck with a boat behind it down the street from the house when I got home this afternoon. It wouldn't have taken but a few minutes for it to get to the church," Tuck responded.

"Okay Lieutenant, I'll do what I can to expedite a forensics team. If this turns out to be murder, we will need to get you folks on that boat and out of here quickly. There are a set of IDs for each of you that you can travel on which should keep anyone off your trail until we get this situation resolved," Morris shook Tuck's hand, ending the conversation.

Tuck returned to the ER waiting where Bob, Kathryn, and Hanna were consoling each other. Hanna ran to him and threw her arms around her husband, now the only man in her life.

"Oh Michael, my heart feels like it is going to break," she sobbed.

"I know Hon, but we need to be strong right now for Kathryn," Tuck said quietly while he gently kissed her forehead, "She is going to need our strength to get through the next couple of weeks."

Hanna just sobbed her heart out as they stood together in silence for the next few minutes.

A young doctor came into the room and quietly announced to Kathryn that they were going to move Harry's body so an FBI forensics team could do their investigation. Kathryn walked back into the emergency triage room that held Harry's body and gave him a final farewell kiss. Several of their congregation had come to the E.R. and were waiting for news of their pastor. Bob took Kathryn by the arm and steadied her as she went into the waiting room to give them the heartbreaking report. Tuck walked Hanna to her father's bedside so she could say a tear-filled goodbye, and then they walked slowly to Tuck's truck for the ride back to the house.

Bob and Kathryn came in an hour later, and she went straight to her room, closing the door behind her. Bob found Tuck sitting in the living room with his hands folded and just staring at the floor.

"Where's Hanna?" he asked.

"She is lying down for a bit. We were worried about all of the stress with the baby and all that," Tuck said without looking up.

"Tuck, I'm going to make a phone call and get us some more help. There is a good bit of truth in the old adage, 'there is safety in numbers', and we need some numbers," Bob said quietly.

"I suppose there is, but right now we are kind of running around like chickens with our head cut off, which it has been, metaphorically speaking," Tuck said, "Who did you have in mind?"

"Shaun O'Brien," Was all Bob said.

Tuck just stared at him for a couple of minutes, "Really, Harry told me that Mr. O'Brien was even more ruthless than the feds that we have had to deal with, and, oh, by the way, he is a fed!"

"Shaun thwarted an attempt on Abigail a short while back, and at the same time was instrumental in getting that Agent Kensey sacked and out of our hair," Bob made his case in a straightforward tone.

"I suppose that we could use some help," Tuck grudgingly admitted, "I'd like to meet Maggie's father anyway."

He got up and walked to the bedroom to be with Hanna, but sleep would not come until the wee hours of the morning.

CHAPTER 30

Early the next morning, people from the church, and folks that knew the family started calling in their condolences and stopping by with food. Tuck called the Colonel and explained the situation, and then called Junior Knowles and told him to meet with his temporary supervisor at the law enforcement center in Conway. His plan was to stay close to the house and help with the logistics of setting up the funeral and arranging for accommodations for those family and friends that would be coming from out of town. Hanna had other ideas, however, as she soon let him know.

"Michael, I've been thinking about the boat," She started sweetly, "I want you to move it away from Bucksport."

"Well, The Grande Dunes Marina is a very short drive from here, and I just happen to have a friend that owns a condo with a slip that they are not using. How long do we need to dock it there?" Tuck answered.

"At least until we leave, Michael. I want to stay on the boat with you, but since that psycho found us at Bucksport, it is time to move," Hanna spoke with a determination in her voice that Tuck was not used to.

"I'll make the arrangements Hon. Maybe Bob can help me with the move. I know that Albert will be glad to go along," Tuck gave in with no argument. The truth was, he was as eager as Hanna to get to a place of relative quiet for the night, and the Night Wind was the perfect place to be.

The arrangements for the slip at The Grande Dunes Marina were made in less than an hour, and Tuck recruited Bob to ride up to Bucksport with him. The call was made to Albert who was delighted to help provided that Tuck could pick him up at the house and give him a ride home later that evening.

Under Albert's watchful eye, the Night Wind eased from her slip and slowly navigated the Waccamaw River north past the swing bridge on old Highway 544 in Socastee. With the tide running in their favor, the trip to The Grande Dunes Marina took about three hours, which turned into a three-hour tutorial for Tuck on the art of sailing this classic oceanic cruiser.

In another hour, the shore power was hooked up, and Tuck had logged the boat in with the harbormaster. Now all that was left was to give Albert a ride home, return to Harry's and pick Hanna up, and then spend the rest of the evening relaxing aboard the Night Wind. Tuck relished the thought of getting a good night's sleep, even though he worried about Hanna, and he certainly was going to miss Harry.

Tuck dropped Bob off at the house and then drove Albert back to Conway. On the way back his reverie was interrupted by the ringing of his cell phone.

"Tuck speaking," He answered.

"Lieutenant Tucker, Anthony Morris here. I've got some news regarding Harry's autopsy. Is this a good time?" Special Agent Morris asked.

"Yes sir, I'm by myself for the next twenty minutes or so. What have you found?" Tuck replied.

"Our forensics team found a small red spot under Harry's left arm which may or may not be the insertion point of a cryogenic dart. There is enough concern for us to continue to search for trace amounts of several chemicals that have been used in this manner to induce a heart attack in otherwise healthy adults," Morris explained.

"I thought that those things were just used in bad movies. Do you mean to tell me that they actually exist?" Tuck was incredulous.

"Actually, the CIA has used them since around the early nineteen seventies for special assassinations," Morris explained, "As far as I know, we have not used them, especially on U.S. soil."

"Do you have any idea who would want to kill Harry like this?" Tuck questioned.

"I don't at this time, although I will rule out George Withers. This just doesn't match his M.O. If we do find a chemical that shouldn't be there, we might be able to trace its origins, but that is going to be a long shot," Special Agent Morris answered, "I'll keep you in the loop, but for the next twenty-four hours, you need to be very careful."

"I understand sir, Thank you for the information," Tuck ended the call.

As if worrying about one psychopath wasn't enough, now Tuck would have to try and stay one step ahead of enemies on at least two fronts. It would be best if Hanna didn't know about this now, but Tuck decided to tell Bob, and probably Henry when the big man arrived for his brother's funeral. Tonight he was going to do his best to make certain that Hanna could grieve for her father without worrying about being killed herself.

Tuck was sitting in the cockpit of the Night Wind enjoying his second cup of coffee while Hanna slept in when his cell phone rang.

"Good morning, Tuck. Shaun O'Brien is here and wants to see you when you can get to the house," Bob announced.

"Hanna is still asleep, Bob. Why don't you bring Mr. O'Brien over, and we can meet here?" Tuck asked since he really did not want to wake his wife.

There was a brief silence, and then, "We are on our way. Put some coffee on."

"The pot is fresh. How about stopping and picking up some donuts for old time's sake?" Tuck said with a laugh.

"We're on it. I'll be there in about twenty minutes," Bob ended the call.

When Shaun O'Brien got out of the car with Bob Pike, Tuck observed that he carried himself like a professional, much like the many mercenaries that he had met in Iraq and Afghanistan. There was something dangerous about these people that worked in the shadows of the government, doing mop-up work for the various secret agencies that needed them. He waved to the two men and motioned for them to come aboard.

"Good morning, Tuck, this is Pastor O'Brien from our work in Honduras," Bob introduced him in a loud voice for the benefit of any listening ears or devices as he handed a dozen mixed donuts to Tuck.

"Glad to meet you, sir," Tuck exclaimed while shaking the big man's hand.

"The pleasure is all mine, Lieutenant Tucker. I knew your father, by the way. We had a few dealings when I had the salvage business years ago down in Georgetown," O'Brien said cordially.

"Just call me Tuck," Tuck responded with a smile.

The men took seats in the cockpit with Tuck as he poured coffee for them.

"Bob has told me about what has been going on up here, Tuck, and I heard some of it through other channels as well. I'd like to help get you all out of here if you will let me," O'Brien said as he leaned forward and lowered his voice.

"Any help would be welcome Mr. O'Brien. This has been a bit of a rough patch for my wife and me. Right now, there is something else that I need to tell you both that I learned last night on the way home. Anthony Morris called me with the preliminary results of Harry's autopsy, and it looks like he may have been poisoned with a cryogenic dart!" Tuck exclaimed in a very low voice to keep from waking his wife.

Bob and Shaun exchanged looks, and then Shaun O'Brien said, "Let's keep this to ourselves while I do some leg work here. I made a real enemy for you folks when I didn't kill Kensey down in

Honduras. It may be that he is behind Harry's death, even though he couldn't be that mobile yet. I do know that his rope has been severely shortened, and his aspirations to climb the agency ladder have been curtailed. He certainly would be the type to come after the family for revenge, or I'm not a good judge of character."

"What do you want us to do?" Bob asked.

"Keep your radar on and act normal. I'll be watching a lot of things during the next few days, and I think that Anthony Morris will be very diligent for your sakes also. By the way, Anthony and I are old friends. He worked an assignment with me in Iraq a few years back that didn't go so well, but he is okay in my book," Shaun concluded.

Tuck knew of a very dark op that had gone horribly wrong while he was there but did not speak of it to Shaun O'Brien.

They engaged in small talk for a few minutes while they finished their coffee and donuts, and then Bob announced that they had to get back to the house. Shaun made mention that he was meeting his daughter for lunch for the first time in years. They shook hands and departed.

"Who was that, Michael?" a small voice came from the galley.

"Bob was here with Maggie O'Brien's father," Tuck answered as he made his way down the companionway to hug his wife.

"Well, I would like to have seen Mr. O'Brien, Tuck. He seemed so mysterious when we were in school," Hanna said.

"You'll get the chance; Hon. I think he will be spending some time with us until we leave," Tuck said as Hanna grew a puzzled look.

"I saved a little coffee and a chocolate donut that Bob brought," Tuck said with a smile, "But you have to hurry up so we can get back over and help Kathryn."

"Aye, aye, Captain Spanky," She saluted and smiled.

Tuck just gave her a big kiss and a hug, and then went back up the companionway to get her coffee and donut.

CHAPTER 31

Henry Albright arrived late that afternoon after an eleven-hour flight from Seattle. He had a sadness about him that told Tuck how much the passing of his brother weighed on him.

"Hello, Tuck," Henry's booming voice sounded a bit weak.

"Hello, Henry, I hope you had a decent flight over. I just wish it could have been under more pleasant circumstances," Tuck replied after getting a bear hug from the big man that took his breath.

"I certainly didn't figure on having to bury Harry this soon, Tuck. He always seemed to be the rock of the family. We are sure going to miss him," Henry's voice broke a bit as he talked about his brother, but he quickly regained his composure.

"It came as a shock to us also, Henry. Hanna is taking it very hard, and I'm worried about Kathryn. She doesn't seem to grasp that Harry is gone yet, and we are afraid that when she does...well you know," Tuck told him, "I need to talk to you in private when you get settled. Something important has come to light where Harry's death is concerned."

"Let me see what all has to be done here tonight, and we'll get together at the hotel later, if that suits you," Henry responded with a puzzled look on his face.

"Uncle Henry!" Hanna came into the room with her sisters and all of them swarmed their favorite and only uncle like little children. Since he was pushed to the outer part of the circle, Tuck took advantage of the opportunity to walk out on the porch where Bob Pike was sitting, listening to the wind driven surf a few blocks from the house.

"Hanna loves the sound of the night wind, Bob. She had several wind chimes up until Harry took them down for a hurricane that never came through," Tuck said quietly.

"This is a nice time of the evening, Tuck. It's a shame that Harry isn't here to enjoy it with us. This porch was his favorite place," Bob replied.

"I have a good feeling about Harry. Where he is now is a heck of a lot better than where we are, my friend," Tuck said with a little humor in his voice.

"Amen to that, Tuck. Have you thought about when we can get ready to leave? I feel like we all need to put some distance between us and Myrtle Beach pretty soon now," Bob asked.

"Hanna will need a week after the funeral to say her goodbyes. We can run the ditch down to McClellanville and then outside to Mayport, Florida. I'm thinking that we will run from there to Fort Lauderdale, and then to Miami before making the run across to Honduras. I've got charts on board, but really haven't made any concrete plans yet," Tuck said.

"Good thinking, Tuck. If you don't have a set plan it will be hard for anyone to anticipate where you will turn up," Bob agreed.

"I'm going to tell Henry about what the FBI found during Harry's autopsy, Bob. He needs to know what we are facing here."

"I agree, Tuck. Henry pissed off a few of those folks further up the rope than any of us. What do you think that he will do?" Bob asked.

"I imagine that he will want a piece of whoever attacked his brother. I certainly would, and Henry is a lot meaner than I am," Tuck said quietly, "I'm going back inside for a bit and see if I can be of any help to Kathryn."

The rest of the evening was spent in remembering Harry. Tomorrow would be the final goodbyes, but tonight there were stories to tell in Harry's memory. Henry was one of the last to hug Kathryn and tell her good night. Bob and Tuck followed him back to the hotel.

Henry sat for a bit after hearing Tuck tell about their suspicions relating to Harry's death. Finally, he stood up and asked, "Do the feds have any ideas about who might have killed him?"

"Not that they are telling, Henry, but Anthony Morris is in our camp on this one. I do think that he will go hard after this if some of those toxins are found in Harry's blood," Tuck said somberly, "I don't want Hanna to know about this because of the added stress that it would put on her and the baby."

"I understand, Tuck. There was something else that I wanted to talk to you about also. If this Honduras venture doesn't work out for you guys, I have a friend in West Texas that will give you cover until after the baby is born. They sure won't think to look for you out there either!" Henry added.

"Well, at least that gives you an alternative if plan 'A' fails," Bob said halfheartedly. He certainly wanted Tuck and Hanna in Honduras with him and Abigail, especially since the baby would be here soon.

"Well, look at it as Plan 'B" then," Henry said, "I'll make a couple of calls and tentatively set things up just in case the other plan goes by the board, as plans sometimes do. I'm going to talk to Agent Morris after the funeral and get his take on what may have killed Harry. If there is any way that I can run interference while I'm here, just let me know."

"We will, Henry. I'll see you in the morning," Tuck said as he stood up to leave.

When he and Bob were outside of the room, Bob spoke, "I'd hate to be on Henry's bad side. I remember how he handled that Richards trouble."

"Yep, Uncle Henry is one of a kind all right, but I think that this is too big for him to handle by himself. I just hope that he stays out of trouble while he is here," Tuck replied.

"I think that Morris will get him settled down. Henry has a history with him, and I think that Morris knows more about what went on the night Richards passed than he lets on," Bob said with a smile.

"You're probably right, Bob. I'm going to pick up Hanna and head for the boat. This has been a long day. You know, I haven't heard one word from the Colonel since I gave my notice. Maybe I should call him tomorrow."

"Better let sleeping dogs lie, my friend," Bob said with a laugh.

"You're probably right, as usual. They apparently have someone watching over our old territory or I would have gotten a call by now," Tuck responded with a short laugh.

He and Bob had been together for a couple of years now, and Tuck had a lot of respect for his ex-partner's viewpoints. Tomorrow was going to be a long and emotionally painful day for Hanna and her family, and Tuck didn't want anything to pull him away from her, especially the Colonel.

They arrived at Harry's and Tuck asked Bob to send Hanna out. He didn't want to get trapped in the crowd of mourners again so he waited in the truck until Hanna came out.

"Hi Babe," He greeted her when she opened the truck door.

"I am so tired, Michael. Let's get to the boat so I can get off my feet," She responded.

We'll be there in a few minutes, Hanna. How are your sisters taking all of this?" Tuck asked.

"We all are still kind of in shock, but Daddy always told us that no man knows the hour that he will be taken. He also said that we shouldn't fret over an early passing because God is in absolute control of our lives and may have saved us from something more evil if we had lived. I want to believe that, but I am going to miss him for a long time," By the time she had finished, Hanna was crying softly.

Tuck reached across the console of the truck and took her hand, "I love you, Hanna. If there is any way to make this less painful, please let me help."

"I love you too, but he was my only Daddy, Michael. Do you remember how it felt to lose your parents?" Hanna responded.

That question hit a nerve with Tuck because the loss of his parents, coupled with the time that he had spent in combat, had dulled his ability to feel emotional pain in the way that most did.

"I remember feeling empty, that's about it," Tuck said simply.

"Oh Michael, I wish that I could fix you inside. I want to see you love and play with your son like other fathers do," Hanna had a worried tone in her voice.

"Don't worry, Hanna. I'm going to love him just as much as I love you. I promise!" He gave her hand a little squeeze to boost her confidence in his remark, although he didn't believe it very strongly himself.

Tuck was glad to get to the marina so that this conversation could stop. One place where he didn't like people, even Hanna, to visit was his neatly packed and padlocked emotional cabinet. There would be time to unlock that door later if they survived.

Tuck helped Hanna up the gangway to the aft deck of the Night Wind and then went below to check everything out before she came down. He noticed that there was some water on the deck just past the galley, and made a mental note to give the boat a thorough inspection in the morning. Hanna came down behind him and went straight to their berth forward of the galley and lounge area.

"I'll be down in a minute, Hon," Tuck said to her as he made his was back topside, "I want to make certain everything is secure before turning in."

"Okay, but hurry up. I need to cuddle," Hanna said with a laugh.

Tuck moved around the deck slowly, conducting a close inspection of the deck and the mooring lines. As he approached the aft deck from the portside, he noticed wet tracks starting at the midships rail and continuing to the cabin. Someone had been on board, and had come in from the waterside to be un-noticed!

Tuck called the number that Shaun O'Brien had given him for emergencies. When the big man answered, Tuck said,

"Hello Shaun, I'm sorry to bother you at this time of night, but someone has been on the boat, and I was wondering if you might have been doing some recon up here?"

"No Tuck, I've been with my daughter Maggie most of the night. Is there anything missing, or damaged?" O'Brien replied.

"No sir, just wet tracks around the deck and down into the galley," Tuck said in a low tone so Hanna wouldn't hear.

"I don't believe that anyone other than George Withers would do something spectacular like an incendiary attack dockside, Tuck, and that is not his M.O. I'll be over first thing in the morning with some equipment, and we will give the old girl a thorough check."

"Shaun, I appreciate this very much. The coffee will be on when you get here," Tuck ended the call and felt relieved that a skilled CIA operative would help him. That is, he felt relieved until he turned around and Hanna was standing there with her arms folded, and a scowl on her pretty face.

"Really Michael...are you keeping any other secrets from me that I need to know about? Who was on our boat and what did they want?" Hanna was in a pretty foul mood, and the only thing Tuck could do was to tell her the truth.

"We need to talk, but not here. Let's go below and I'll tell you everything that we have found out since Harry's death. I didn't want to tell you all of this because of the baby and all of the stress of the last few days, but since you already know some of it, I'll give you the whole story," Tuck said as he gently guided her to the companionway and down to the galley where he turned the radio on and cranked the volume up. Over two bowls of 'Death by Chocolate' ice cream, Tuck told Hanna everything they knew or suspected about Harry's death and the fact that there was more than one person still trying to kill them. He also told her about Shaun O'Brien, and his willingness to help them get out of the area safely.

Hanna just sat and listened wide-eyed until Tuck brought his narrative to a close, and then just said,

"I feel better now Michael. It might just be the ice cream, but somehow I know that you are doing all that you can to protect us, you, me, and the baby. Let's go to bed."

With that, she got up from the galley table, rinsed her bowl, and went to bed. Tuck followed closely with a feeling of immense relief that he wouldn't be keeping secrets from Hanna anymore.

CHAPTER 32

Shaun O'Brien was true to his word and showed up bright and early the next morning while Hanna and Tuck were having breakfast in the aft deck cabin. With him was his red-haired reporter daughter, Maggie O'Brien! As they neared the gangway, Hanna waved to Maggie and gave her a big smile. Shaun was behind Maggie, and he gave Tuck a shrug of defeat to let him know that she had bullied him into bringing her along.

"Hanna, I am so sorry about your father," Maggie said as she gave Hanna a sisterly hug.

"Thank you, Maggie. I'm glad that you came over. Can I pour you all some coffee?" Hanna offered graciously.

"That would be great, Hanna. After coffee, I am going to take you to the house while these men do whatever it is that they are going to do," Maggie said with a big smile. Hanna would be her captive for a couple of hours anyway. What an opportunity!

"Tuck, I've got that equipment in the car, if you can give me a hand," Shaun was up and off the boat followed closely by Tuck.

"I'm really sorry about bringing Maggie, Tuck, but you know how she is," Shaun apologized.

"No need for an apology, Shaun. Hanna needs a woman to talk to, and Maggie feels like I snubbed her during the cougar incidents. Well the coy-wolf and bear incidents also and maybe one or two other minor things along the way," Tuck told her father with a big grin on his face.

The truth was, he had made a game out of messing with any of the reporters, especially Maggie O'Brien.

"She doesn't know anything about what I'm doing here, except that I am going to survey your boat. Once she and Hanna leave, we'll see what our nefarious friend might have been up to last night," Shaun said quietly so that Maggie wouldn't overhear.

The two men carried four waterproof aluminum cases back to the boat and sat them on the aft deck before returning to their coffee. Hanna and Maggie had gone below so the men had the cockpit to themselves. Tuck showed Shaun where the footprints started, and where they went down the companionway, but they were soon interrupted by the girls coming back up. Hanna had changed clothes, and gave Tuck a big hug before announcing,

"Maggie and I are going to run over to Akel's for a big breakfast before we go to the house. You two have fun."

Tuck just gave her a big smile and said, "Be careful, Hanna."

As soon as they had left the parking lot, Tuck and Shaun started unpacking his equipment, which consisted of several types of tracking equipment, a signal jammer, and a sniffer for detecting several types of military grade explosives. The most interesting one to Tuck was the little hand held GPS tracking device detector that Shaun turned on right after the signal-jamming device.

"Well, that didn't take long!" Shaun exclaimed, "Somebody is broadcasting your GPS co-ordinates, Tuck."

"Can you find the source?" Tuck asked.

"Yep, give me a minute or two to triangulate the signal," He said as he made his was along the starboard side of the boat.

At just forward of midships, Shaun stopped abruptly and turned back toward Tuck. He stopped again and raised his arm skyward toward the mast.

"There it is, Tuck! They are using your antenna to broadcast a signal, probably under any other bandwidth that you are using so that it wouldn't be noticed," Shaun explained the situation, "Now that we know where that one is, let's have a look around below decks."

They unpacked the explosive sniffer, a small gadget that looked like a miniature vacuum cleaner complete with a small hose and a filter of some sort attached to the end.

Once in the galley area, the detector started chirping softly with the intensity increasing as they made their way forward. When they had come to the trunk of the main mast, the device was signaling wildly that there was something amiss. Shaun looked at his readings and then stooped to pull up the deck boards covering the shallow bilge. Just under the mast was a small satchel type of waterproof case that housed two pounds of Semtech explosive and a cell phone trigger.

"Wow, this is really a professional job, Tuck. Take a look," Shaun exclaimed as he moved aside so that Tuck could see the handiwork of a master bomb maker.

Tuck was not a novice when it came to defusing explosive ordinance, but this one looked far more sophisticated than the IEDs that he had experienced in Iraq and Afghanistan.

"It looks like someone is planning on giving you a real "Bon-Voyage' party when you get far enough offshore so that no one will notice," Brian said with a deadly serious expression on his face, "but I think that you will be safe enough until you get out of sight of land. As screwed up as some of our federal agencies are, even they won't blow up half of this marina to kill you."

"That's not much consolation, Shaun. What do you suggest that we do?" Tuck asked.

"Leave the Semtech in place. At least we know where this one is. If we tamper with it, they will know, and we might not find the next one. Hell boy, I'd give them exactly what they wanted! Let's get this gear put up, and then go someplace and plan where we don't have to have that jammer running. If that is on too long, someone will get suspicious."

"I hear that little place on the beach has some great Belgium waffles," Tuck suggested.

"Sounds good, nothing makes me hungrier than plotting against the government!" O'Brien exclaimed with a laugh as he clapped Tuck on the shoulder.

By ten o'clock, Shaun and Tuck had a plan put together, and it was time to get ready for Harry's going home celebration. The church was packed with people standing in the foyer and lining the sidewalk outside to pay their respects to their friend and pastor. After the service, the congregation followed the hearse and the family to the graveside where the local VFW Honor Guard gave Harry a full military burial complete with a seven-gun salute, a trumpet rendition of taps, and then a Scotsman in full dress played 'Amazing Grace' on his bagpipes.

Tuck leaned over to Hanna and whispered softly, "Harry would really have enjoyed this."

She responded by just shaking her head in the affirmative as the tears ran down her cheeks.

Tuck had been watching the crowd, and he noticed that several of the men that attended the funeral were paying more attention to the crowd than the service.

"Good old Special Agent Morris," He thought.

It looked like the man was going to protect the family, as much as was possible until they were able to leave.

The most moving part of the ceremony was the VFW Honor Guard folding Harry's flag and handing it to Kathryn. There wasn't a dry eye in the house, including Tuck's, which surprised him...more than a little.

The church congregation had arranged for a large barbeque in Harry's honor following the graveside service, and it gave Tuck the ideal opportunity to let Hanna and Bob in on the change in their plans. The objections were numerous, to say the least.

"Well, I don't like the idea of riding a bomb down the inter-coastal anymore than you all do, but if we go offshore, somebody is likely to ring that number and evaporate us," Tuck explained as he tried to smooth the objections of his crew.

"Michael, are you certain that they won't blow us up in the waterway?" Hanna asked with concern.

"Ninety-nine percent sure, Hon. Shaun says that we are safer with the bomb on board than if we removed it," Tuck answered.

"Tuck, how are you going to get that thing out away from innocent people without getting yourself killed?" Bob asked. He didn't like the idea of riding on the top of the Semtech any better than Hanna, but it did seem like a better plan to deal with a known danger than to have to face another unknown and possibly bigger threat later.

"Bob, I haven't worked out any of the details yet, but we will have time as we run the ditch down to McClellanville to come up with a workable idea," Tuck hoped he sounded confident, "Special Agent Morris has offered us fake identities to travel on, and I think that we can put them to good use. We also have a good bit of cash set aside to travel on. Everything is going to be fine."

"Okay Michael, I trust you to take care of us," Hanna said as she leaned over and gave him a sloppy barbeque kiss, and then got up and went over to talk to her sisters.

"Tuck, we've got a week before we leave. Do you think that Hanna can sleep on that bomb for that long without spilling the beans?" Bob sounded worried.

"Well, I kind of thought that you and I would stay on the boat so Hanna could spend the next week with Kathryn," Tuck sprung that with a grin.

"I might have known!" Bob laughed as he got up and started for the barbeque, "You know what they say, eat drink and be merry..."

CHAPTER 33

Luckily, for George Withers, he still had several contacts within the Bureau that answered his calls. One of those calls got him a new car and another identity so that he could finally travel back to Myrtle Beach in relative anonymity. He had heard about the death of Harry Albright through the local news, but had little interest in the event other than it brought more scrutiny on the family, and made it harder to get close to his assignment, Hanna Tucker. He would shadow them for the next week and look for an opportunity, even if it meant killing her husband.

George drove back into Myrtle Beach on the day of Harry's funeral looking like a tourist and took a room under his new alias, James (Jimmy) Bledsoe from Philadelphia. He planned on spending the next couple of days riding through the neighborhood where Hanna was staying on the pretext of buying a retirement home. Several of the realtors in the area offered that service, and there would be no suspicion raised if he cruised through in a realtor's car. Of course, his plan also included dumping the realtor somewhere a body wouldn't be easy to locate, and then using the car for the next week or so if necessary. Unknown to George was the fact that Tuck and Bob had seen his face on the papers that Al and Teddy had faxed the night that George's friends within the Bureau confiscated them, supposedly unread.

He used the computer terminal in the hotel lobby to search for realtors in the area until he found the right one. A short phone call later, and he had an appointment set up for the next day with Betty Lansing, an independent broker that worked out of her home. Finally, his luck seemed to have changed.

Tuck sat on the porch of the house with Hanna and listened to her talk to her sisters about how much Harry had meant to the family. He wondered if his children would think kindly of him in the same way when he was gone. Harry was a special man and Tuck wanted to be like him for Hanna and the baby, he just didn't know if he was cut out of the same cloth.

"Tuck, are you paying attention?" Hanna asked, jogging him back to reality.

"Sure Babe. What were you saying?" Tuck answered without thinking how dumb that sounded.

"We were talking about how men never pay attention to us, and I was taking your side. Boy was I wrong!" Hanna teased him to the laughter of her sisters.

It was good to hear them get together and share a laugh, especially after going through the loss of their father. Tuck just gave them a smile and drifted back out again. This time, he wondered how Kathryn was going to get along without her soul mate. Tuck had always dismissed that idea until he had met Hanna, and now he knew that there was that 'One' person you were supposed to be with. He felt sympathy for Kathryn and hoped the girls would keep in touch with her.

"I'm going to find Bob," Tuck announced as he got up from the porch swing and went into the house.

Most of the crowd had left, but several of the women were cleaning up the kitchen for Kathryn. Bob was in the living room talking to some of Harry's friends.

"Excuse me, Bob, could I see you in the backyard for a couple of minutes?" Tuck asked.

"Be right there," Bob replied and excused himself from the small group.

Tuck was waiting by the old picnic table that sat alongside the back porch.

"What's up Tuck?" Bob asked as he came out and sat on the top of the table.

"I've been giving this a lot of thought, Bob. When Shaun and I found that bomb this morning, I knew that Hanna and I probably would not be going to Honduras with you. Henry has found us a very secluded place to stay in Odessa, Texas, and I think that I am going to take that option if we don't get blown up beforehand," Tuck told him, "Besides, I'm not ready to give up on this country just yet, in spite of how corrupt our government has become."

"I had a feeling that you probably would make that decision, Tuck. That is why I booked a flight out of Charleston next week under the false identity that Agent Morris provided me," Bob replied to the news.

"Okay, then that makes things easier for us. We will need to make all of our plans away from the boat since it is probably bugged by now. Once we get to McClellanville, we will have to be careful not to be seen by too many people, but hopefully, I can get the Night Wind set up on an outbound course and then get off her before the big boom," Tuck said as he outlined his plan.

"Hmmm... and what happens if you get blown up, or didn't you think that far ahead?" Bob asked sarcastically.

"If something happens, you will have to get Hanna to Honduras under the false identity. Promise me that you will do that for me," Tuck implored.

"Of course, I will, Tuck. That is, I will if Hanna will go along," Bob answered with sincerity.

"I'll talk to Hanna later about the possibility, but not tonight. She has a lot on her plate. We'll, we've got a lot of packing to do in the next couple of days, and some more work on the boat, so I think we'll head out. I believe that Hanna will be all right on the boat for one night. Tomorrow I'll let her stay here with Kathryn," Tuck shook Bob's hand and went to get Hanna.

The next few days passed quickly with much having to be done to get ready to leave. Tuck turned his truck in at the Conway Law Enforcement Center and rode back with Bob in the rental that would be their only transportation from this point.

Hanna and Kathryn shopped for provisions under the ever-watchful eye of the FBI team that was ever present. Unseen, of course, was the team that Shaun O'Brien had organized, but if deadly force had to be met, this was the bunch that would carry the day.

As they all took the opportunity to relax onboard the Night Wind, Tuck talked loudly of the route that they would take in a couple of days when they left Myrtle Beach for Honduras.

"I thought that maybe we would motor down the Waccamaw and stop at Hannah Banana's for a last lunch. Word has it that they will sell soon, so this will be a good time to say good-bye. We'll make Georgetown in the late afternoon and dock at the Georgetown Marina for the night. If we can stand the smell of the paper plant, we'll eat down on the boardwalk. The next day we get up early and head down to McClellanville; spend the night there, and then it's off into the open water for us for about two days. What do you think about that?" Tuck asked everyone when he had finished.

"I think that this is going to be fun," Hanna made a face that belied her words. Hopefully, they weren't being filmed.

"I can hardly wait to feel that salt spray in my face again, Tuck!" Bob chimed in with a laugh.

"Henry has invited me to come out and stay with them for a brief vacation," Kathryn said fighting back tears, "I'm going to do it too. We'll decide about the house and the church when I get back, but I will let you all know what is going on up here. I'm certainly going to miss you both."

"Kathryn, you have been like a mother to me and to Tuck," Hanna said as she gave her a hug, "You have a home with us if you ever need it, and don't think you are going to get out of playing with this baby!"

"Oh Hanna," Was all that Kathryn could muster as she broke into tears.

"Guys, I'm going to ride back to the house with Kathryn. See you in a little while," Hanna announced as they got up to leave.

Tuck gave her a hug, and then turn to Bob and whispered in a very conspiratorial tone, "That was pretty good, don't you think?"

Bob just grimaced and said, "I guess we'll know if we reach McClellanville."

The next two days were spent preparing for the trip. Bob packed a few clothes, and then put the rest of his belongings in a box and shipped them back to Abigail in Honduras. That wouldn't arouse any suspicions since living onboard a sailing vessel required a good bit of austerity. Tuck met with Special Agent Morris who tried to assure him that they were doing everything possible to uncover the identity of the second killer. The old question that had nagged at him on the drive back from Columbia finally made sense so he presented it to Morris.

"Is it possible that this continued attack on my wife and Harry's death are actually sanctioned by the FBI?" he asked Morris.

There was silence for a minute, and then, "Tuck, I'm afraid that even I don't have an answer for you on that. I wish that I could dismiss your question with a resounding 'No Way!', but I am not privy to all of the dark secrets of the people that I work for. Hell, we have a president that wouldn't hesitate to use a drone strike on U.S. soil if he thought that he could find a good enough excuse."

"Well, that would explain how Withers has been able to elude capture, wouldn't it?" Tuck pressed for an answer.

"Yes it would Tuck, but that doesn't mean I personally won't do everything humanly possible to keep you and Hanna safe," Special Agent Morris answered as he shook Tuck's hand in dismissal.

"Thank you, sir, I appreciate your candor," Tuck replied as he took his leave of Anthony Morris.

He drove back to the house just in time to see Hanna outside doing some yard work with Kathryn. Tuck parked the car and hurried to where she was standing close to the street.

"Hanna, what in the world are you doing?" Tuck asked in a serious tone.

"It's okay Michael. I'm just helping Kathryn clean up these pinecones. We'll be through in a few minutes," She replied.

"I don't care about the pine cones," Tuck practically shouted back, "I care about you making a target of yourself right before we leave this place!"

As he finished his little tirade, Tuck looked up and noticed a car driving slowly up the street. On its door was a magnetic sign that read 'Betty Lansing, Independent Real Estate Broker'. As the car pulled up close to them, Tuck's senses went on high alert. There was something familiar with the man that was in the passenger seat

"Hanna get in the house and call 911 quick! It's George Withers!" Tuck Exclaimed as he reached into his back pocket for the LCP 9 Ruger that he had started carrying. Withers looked directly at Tuck, and, realizing that his cover was blown, reached his foot across the console of Betty Lansing's car and pressed the accelerator down with her foot pinned under his. He grabbed the wheel with his left hand, released the latch on her seat belt with his right hand, and then reached across her, opened the door and pushed her out of the car in the middle of a sharp curve in the road. Betty hit the ground screaming in pain and panic as Tuck loosed three rounds of nine-millimeter hollow points at the fast moving car.

The unmarked car that had been on the side street finally came sliding to a stop beside Tuck who was now running to where Betty was lying in the neighbor's yard, crying.

"What are you shooting at?" The driver demanded.

"George Withers! He just made a drive by and threw this woman out of the car!" Tuck responded angrily, "You're wasting time sitting here. Try to catch him!"

The two FBI agents left in pursuit of Withers, if they actually were pursuing him, and directly behind them came the Myrtle Beach Police, sirens howling and lights flashing. Bob was now in the road with Tuck, and he handled the police while Tuck went into the house with Hanna.

"Hanna, don't you ever do that to me again!" Tuck shouted.

Hanna was crying and Kathryn was patting her on the back.

"Tuck, you leave this poor girl alone!" Kathryn demanded, "She was trying to help me. If you want to shout at anyone, blame me and not her."

"I'm sorry Hanna. It's just that if I had been a few minutes later, you might have been his victim," Tuck apologized.

His cell phone rang before Hanna could answer.

"Tuck, Anthony Morris here. I have a report that there was an attempt made on Hanna. My men have located the car, but Withers has escaped," Morris said.

"There was something funny about the time that it took for your men to get here, Agent Morris. They didn't seem too interested in making the pursuit either, which kind of confirms what we talked about," Tuck responded angrily.

"I'm sorry Tuck, but I will provide you with everything that you need to make this trip happen. Let me know if there is anything else that I can do," Morris seemed sincere.

"I will sir. Right now I'm going to take care of my wife," Tuck said and then ended the call.

George Withers ditched the car behind the Pirates Cove Putt Putt course and ran across Kings Highway to Ocean Drive where he had left his car earlier that morning before walking back to his hotel and waiting for Betty Lansing to pick him up. There would be no going back to the hotel now, so he decided that his best bet would be to wait in McClellanville for the Night Wind to dock in the next couple of days as his contacts informed him that she would. This would be his last chance to fulfill his contract, and this time, he was determined not to fail.

CHAPTER 34

The day of their departure had arrived at last, and a small Bon Voyage party was held at the gangway of the Night Wind by the few well-wishers that had come to see them off. Kathryn was teary eyed as she hugged Hanna and Tuck good-bye, as were several friends of the pair including Anthony Morris, who slipped a packet of papers into Bob Pike's hand unobserved.

Tuck looked up as the WLIB news van pulled up and Maggie O'Brien stepped out with her cameraman.

"Hi Hanna!" she exclaimed gleefully as they set up directly in the front of the gangway for a feature story on the wildlife hero and his wife sailing to Honduras with Bob Pike, a veteran of the DNR.

"Hi Maggie, what's up with the camera crew?" Tuck asked suspiciously.

Maggie leaned in and said in a conspiratorial whisper, "Daddy's idea, Michael, just play along."

Tuck was surprised but did not show it as they spent the next thirty minutes detailing for the nightly news the exact plans that they had made for the trip that they would soon be leaving on.

After the show ended, Maggie dismissed the cameraman and came aboard the Night Wind to hug Hanna and wish her Godspeed on her trip.

"I've got a big surprise myself, Hanna," She said with a big smile breaking out on her face, "In about two weeks, start watching Fox Nightly News and you will see a new 'Fair and Balanced' reporter."

"You're kidding, right?" Hanna asked in surprise, "I mean you're certainly pretty enough, but I didn't think that I would ever know a real celebrity."

"Congratulations, Maggie. If you think reporting on killer animals was hard, just wait until you start putting pressure on those Capitol Hill politicians!" Tuck exclaimed with a laugh.

"Well you two, best of luck, and don't forget me if you have another big story to report," Maggie said as she hugged them both and then left the boat.

Tuck fired up the Perkins Diesel and let it warm up while the rest of the goodbyes were said. Just before they cast off the lines and eased out of the slip, a dark blue Ford sedan roared into the marina parking lot with blue lights flashing and the siren wailing. It was Detectives Teddy Loveless and Al Banks from Columbia.

"Hey Tuck," Teddy shouted as they ran toward the dock, "You didn't mean to leave without saying goodbye did you?"

Tuck stepped over the rail and onto the dock to shake hands with Al and Teddy who had come all of the way from Columbia to see him off.

"Why didn't you guys tell me that you were coming down? I might have missed you," Tuck said with a big grin. He had really come to appreciate these two men and the sacrifice that they were ready to make for him.

"We wanted to surprise you, Tuck. Here's a little something for the trip," Al said as he handed Tuck a manila envelope.

"Thanks, guys. That information that you faxed probably saved Hanna's life the other day," Tuck told them.

"We heard. That's why we brought the envelope. Captain Grays said that he would deny it if anyone said so, but he sent us with it. It has everything we have on George Withers, including some decent pictures," Teddy said.

"Keep in touch, Tuck. We might need someplace to vacation in if you know what I mean," Al said as he gave Tuck's hand a vigorous shake.

"I'll be in touch as soon as everything gets straightened out guys. Thanks so much," Tuck shook their hands and returned to the boat as Bob cast off the dock lines, and Hanna backed her slowly and expertly out into the basin with a long blast on the horn signaling their departure.

"Next stop Hannah Banana's!" Tuck announced as they swung out into the main channel of the Intercoastal Waterway and headed south.

"Try not to hit any bumps, Hanna dear," He chided as she kicked the throttle up to a four-knot cruise.

Hanna just stuck her tongue out at him and said, "Aye, aye, Captain!"

Bob and Tuck sat on the forward cabin and watched for any suspicious activity from both the water and the shoreline. Their nerves were taught as they rode the top of a two-pound bomb that could be set off at any moment. It was a big gamble that they were taking, but a necessary risk if they were to arrive at their destinations in one piece.

After thirty minutes, Tuck went aft to relieve Hanna at the helm.

"I'm going to lie down for a little bit," She told him, "Wake me up if something interesting happens."

Tuck gave her a kiss, but thought to himself, "What could be more interesting that riding an IED down the river on a sunny day?"

They soon came into Socastee and radioed the swing bridge for passage. After a ten minute wait, the bridge opened and they motored slowly toward Bucksport. As the marina came into view, Bob waved to Tuck and pointed to a small boat that was skipping across the water toward them. It was George Tomlinson, the Dock Master, coming to bid them farewell.

"Ahoy the Night Wind," He called as he pulled alongside.

Tuck pulled the throttle back and reduced speed until they were just drifting slowly in the current.

"Hello, George!" Tuck shouted

"Hello Tuck, Bob. I heard that you were coming down this way and wanted to say good-bye to you all. Who knows when we might get together again?" George said as he stood in the small boat with his hand on the side of the Night Wind.

If Tuck was surprised that George knew they were on the way, he didn't show it.

"George, it's been good knowing you, and I do appreciate you 'fixing' the deal on this boat," Tuck said with a smile.

George reached up and took his hand in a firm grasp, "Fair weather to you, son, and to those that sail with you."

With that, Tuck waved good-bye and stepped back to the helm. George stood waving in his boat as the Night Wind picked up speed in the south flowing current and slowly disappeared around the next bend in the river.

It was just after twelve noon when they rounded the turn and saw Richmond Island, and the Wacca Wache Marina come into view. Tuck radioed the Marina for permission to dock which was granted. With the south flowing tide, Tuck had to pass the marina and then turn to bring it up on their starboard side. He eased the boat up to the dock and Bob passed the bowline to the dock master who tied it off to a cleat. Once that was done, Tuck cut the throttle and let the current set the boat into the dock. Then he secured the stern line. Hanna came up from below deck, and the three made their way to the cabana for a light lunch, and to say goodbye to their old friends. Tuck had that old unsettled feeling as they were walking in, and turned in time to catch a glint of sunlight reflected off something shiny in the wooded swamp of Richmond Island.

"Bob, don't turn around, but we are being watched," He said to Bob Pike.

"As long as it's not through a scope, I'm good," Bob replied.

Hanna just looked at Tuck with a bit of fear in her eyes, and Tuck gave her hand a squeeze of reassurance. One thing was certain; someone was tracking them and most likely reporting on their every move. They would have to be careful in their actions and conversations if their plans were to work out.

All three breathed a sigh of relief when they were underway again. The rumors that they had heard about the impending sale of Hannah Banana's turned out to be true, so they were not the only ones in transition.

Tuck called the Georgetown Marina in Georgetown, South Carolina to book a slip for the night. He gave an ETA of around five o'clock that evening to allow for the tide, which was beginning to turn to the north. They would lay in there for the night and experience a little of the River Walk atmosphere just as if they were really tourists. Besides, the food in some of the establishments along the river was excellent as long as the wind kept the worst of the paper mill smell out of their noses.

As they eased into the Sampit River toward Georgetown Marina, Tuck pointed out the many alligators that lay along the banks of the island just off to their port side. It was certainly going to be a change to live in the desert where those types of animals didn't exist, he thought to himself.

When they had docked and made arrangements with the dock master for fuel, they walked down Front Street to Portafino's Restaurant. As they were being seated, a large framed man caught Bob's eye and motioned him to the side. Bob excused himself and acted as if he was going to the men's room.

"Shaun...what are you doing here?" Bob asked in amazement.

"You need to tell Tuck to be very alert when you get to McClellanville. George Withers is down there waiting for the boat to dock, and it is pretty apparent that someone is feeding him information. Now act like you're just coming back from the restroom, and give Tuck the info quietly. I can't be seen here just in case you are being tailed," Shaun explained quickly and then slipped out.

Bob continued to the restroom and then returned to the table. As he was seating himself, Tuck leaned in and asked in a whisper, "What did Shaun want?"

"Withers is in McClellanville. We need to be very alert tomorrow," Bob answered.

"Well like a good friend of mine said the other night, 'eat drink and be merry'..." Tuck responded with a smile.

Hanna was distracted by the decorations in the restaurant and missed the conversation, to Tuck's relief.

When they returned to the boat, the gnats were so annoying on the waterfront, that they immediately went below deck and were surprised to find a bag that contained a bottle of 'Avon Skin So Soft' lotion and three burner phones with a note:

"The lotion is for the gnats, and the phones are for comms from here out. Call me when you reach Goat Island above McClellanville. Shaun"

Tuck passed out the phones and collected their old ones, which he put in his rucksack, but not before smearing some of the lotion on the back of his neck, hands and arms. Hanna followed suit as did Bob.

"I can't believe that we forgot about the darned gnats, Tuck, after all of the time we've spent on the water. Let's get an early start and hopefully the deer flies won't be biting before we get to South Island and the ditch," Bob said when they were topside.

Tuck laughed at his ex-partner, "You're exactly right, Bob. I completely forgot about the most irritating part of this trip, the gnats, and deer flies."

"Good old Shaun," Hanna pitched in, "I wish that Maggie had been able to spend more time with him. She certainly has a few of his traits."

"Well, he is a good man, although he certainly does some hard things. It's difficult to think of him as a pastor, but he does that well also," Bob added.

"I'm glad that he's on our side," Tuck replied, "tomorrow we will need all of the help we can get. Once we are in the waterway, Bob, I'm going to need for you to take the helm while I try and get ready to meet Mr. Withers. By the way, we need to stand guard tonight; do you want the first watch?"

"Suites me, Tuck, I'll wake you up at midnight or thereabouts," Bob replied.

"I'll bring up my .45 and put it in the cabin. You never know about these folks that are shadowing us," Tuck said as he and Hanna went below.

Tuck felt a hand shaking him gently awake and he silently got up so as not to wake Hanna. Bob was standing in the dark galley.

"What time is it, Bob?" Tuck asked sleepily.

"Just after two am. I thought I'd let you sleep a little longer. Things are pretty quiet, but there is a car in the parking lot that has someone lighting a cigarette every thirty minutes or so...probably our friends," Bob said.

"I'll keep an eye on them. Thanks, Bob," Tuck said as he went topside and took his watch until sunrise.

Hanna awoke to the smell of coffee brewing and bacon sizzling on the galley stove.

"What time is it?" she asked groggily.

"Six a.m., Love, time to rise and shine," Tuck said, "How many eggs can you eat?"

"Four!" Bob's voice came from the forward berths.

Hanna laughed and said, "I just want one egg this morning, Tuck. That and the coffee will do me for a while."

"Someone else can be the galley slave tomorrow!" Tuck said loudly for the benefit of anyone listening.

They finished breakfast quickly and Tuck went to the office to settle the tab for the night's dockage and the diesel top off. He had a good chuckle at the sight of the two men in the undercover sedan that we busily engaged in changing the two rear tires that had mysteriously gone flat during the night.

Bob had the Perkins fired up when Tuck stepped back onboard.

"Cast off the lines Bob. We're underway," Tuck called as he cast off the stern line and let the tide swing the stern away from the dock. A long blast on the horn signaled that they were backing out into the channel, and soon they were on their way down Winyaw Bay to the South Island entrance of the Intercoastal waterway also known as 'the ditch'.

The flies weren't that bad at high tide, but there were a few. Bob secured the drops on the cabin in an effort to keep them out, but the morning sun soon made a closed cabin uncomfortably warm.

"We'll have to open her up when we get to South Island, Tuck, flies, or no flies," Bob said.

"I'm thinking that they won't be a problem until low tide, Bob. By then we should be close to McClellanville," Tuck replied.

He hoped that was the case because the deer fly had a particularly nasty bite that drew blood, and stung like the dickens.

Remarkably, the flies seemed to disappear when they made the turn behind Middle Ground at the South Island light. Bob opened the boat back up and Hanna came on deck.

"How long until we have to contact Shaun?" she asked Tuck.

"Well, the tide will start falling in about thirty minutes, so we will be bucking it for awhile until we get further down the waterway. I'm thinking maybe an hour, maybe an hour and a half," Tuck responded.

They were just passing the South Island Ferry on the starboard side so the trip down the waterway had only just begun. Bob came back aft and took the helm from Tuck as he went into the cabin and unpacked the .308 Remington that had been his favorite since his return from duty. He wrapped it in a towel and took it topside to the aft cabin for ready access. Tuck handed Bob the Ruger P-90 and stuck the LCP-9 in his back pocket.

"Hanna, if there is any trouble I want you to get below, all the way forward, and lay down," Tuck said to her in a manner that didn't allow any room for argument.

"Yes Dear," She replied sweetly, but he knew that she wasn't going to hide from a fight.

Shaun's number was programmed into the phone that Tuck had, and he called it as they approached Goat Island.

"Shaun," Was the one-word answer to the call.

"Shaun, it's Tuck. We are just coming up on Goat Island. Have you got eyes on Withers?" Tuck asked.

"I've got him in sight Tuck. Now I want you to promise me that you won't tell Hanna that he is here. Got that?"

"Okay Shaun, I understand. What's the plan?" Tuck answered.

Hanna was looking straight at him as he spoke, but couldn't hear the conversation on the other end.

"Okay, we'll dock the boat and then go get provisions, right?" Tuck answered Shaun and then ended the call.

"What did he say, Tuck? Are we all right?" Hanna had a worried tone in her voice.

"Everything is fine, Babe. We are going to dock, and then go get the rest of our provisions for the trip. Shaun has everything covered."

Hanna gave a sigh of relief and went forward to watch the scenery. Tuck turned to Bob with his back to Hanna so that she couldn't see them talking.

"Withers is there, Bob. Shaun wants us to dock the boat, and then go shopping as if nothing is happening. He wants to use Hanna for bait," Tuck sounded worried.

"I know Shaun, and I think that he is probably the best at what he does. Hanna will be all right if he says so," Bob replied, "Besides, what are the options?"

"You know that I am going to have to kill him, don't you?" Tuck asked speaking of George Withers.

"One of us should, that's for certain," Bob's tone was deadly serious.

The rest of the trip to the marina was as tedious as if they were pulling a long splinter out very slowly. Finally, they saw the docks of McClellanville come into sight, and Tuck's adrenaline started to flood into his body just like the moments before he faced combat. There was no fear now, just the resolve to come out of this intact with his family. His blood seemed like ice in his veins, and he knew that soon he would finally be rid of this man that had brought so much pain to his wife.

They made the turn into the dock that lay perpendicular to the main channel and tied the Night Wind up several empty slips down. Tuck attached the shore power connector and made certain that the lines were secure, and then they waited.

CHAPTER 35

At first, Tuck didn't recognize the old fisherman in the beat up pickup truck that pulled up to the dock edge. When he got out and slowly made his way to the spot where they were docked, he called down, "Are you the folks that needed the ride to the store? Willy sent me to pick you up."

Shaun looked twenty years older than he was, and was dressed in old rain gear and white boots, the trademark of a fisherman.

"That's us!" Tuck called loudly for the benefit of George Withers who had to be nearby, "We'll be right up."

"I'm going to stay with the boat, if that is okay, Michael. I'm really tired, and I think that I am just going to sun on the foredeck until you get back."

Hanna gave Tuck a big hug and a kiss before making her way forward on the boat for a little rest and relaxation while they waited to get started on the last, and possibly the most dangerous, leg of their odyssey. Tuck stepped off onto the dock to join Bob on the supply run.

"I'll be back in about an hour, Hon," He called out as they walked down the dock to the ladder that led to the parking lot where Shaun waited for them. Hanna replied with a wave of her hand.

The gentle rocking of the big West Sail and the warmth of the morning sun soon lulled Hanna into a peaceful nap, one of the few that she had enjoyed since the attempt on their lives by the mysterious killer that they knew only by the reported alias that he sometimes used, George Withers. Oblivious to any activity on the dock, Hanna slipped off into a deep sleep.

Withers, seeing his opportunity, crept out from behind the big dock storage box two slips down from the Night Wind, and made his way swiftly to the stern mooring of the West Sail where Hanna slept. The falling tide had made any visibility from the parking lot to the dock almost impossible, so it was an ideal time for him to finish the contract that he had been hired to do. He pulled the suppressed Ruger target pistol from his bag and had started to step quietly onto the side of the Night Wind when his world turned black and silent.

As his vision returned, George could dimly make out that he was in a seated position in the cabin of the sailboat. He soon became aware that his arms were uncomfortably bound behind him around the trunk of the mast with plastic ties, and that duct tape was wrapped around the top of his head securing him to the mast at that point also. There was a rag of some sort stuck in his mouth and his feet were tied and duct-taped together in front of him. His head pounded from the blow behind his right ear that had rendered him unconscious, and, as his vision cleared, he could make out Tuck and Shaun O'Brien sitting at the galley table watching him intently.

"You should have quit after Conway, George," Tuck spoke when he saw Withers eyes open, "You didn't really think that I was going to let you hurt my wife again, did you?

George's eyes followed Tuck as he spoke, but Withers made no attempt at sound.

"I'll be back in a few minutes George, and then you and I will take a little voyage together," Tuck told him as they made their way up the companionway, and out onto the deck where Bob and Hanna waited.

"Tuck, promise me that you are not going to kill that man!" Hanna was adamant.

"I'm not going to kill him, Hanna. If he dies, it will be the ocean that gets him," Tuck replied in a not very convincing manner, "I need for you to take some of the money that we have and find us an old car. Use the fake papers that Morris gave us, and I'll be back in a couple of hours."

"Tuck, it looks like the weather is turning on you. Are you certain that you can take her out and get back on the dingy before that ocean's up?" Shaun asked.

"I just have to take her out a few miles, Shaun. That little Carib will get me back even if she blows up a bit. Besides, the sea will be at my back, everything will be fine," Tuck tried to reassure his new friend.

"Tuck, do what you feel is right to keep Hanna safe, but keep your conscience safe also," Bob replied as he shook Tuck's hand.

"You sounded a bit like Harry just then," Tuck said with a smile.

Tuck turned and fired up the Perkins diesel as the others gathered on the dock. After releasing the mooring lines, he backed slowly away from the dock and maneuvered the boat to take advantage of the rising tide and deeper water in the channel. Soon he was in Price's Inlet and headed for the open ocean. Tuck picked up the mike on the FM marine band radio, "Charleston Coast Guard, Charleston Coast Guard, this is the sailing vessel 'Night Wind' requesting a radio check, over."

"Sailing Vessel Night Wind, this is the Charleston Coast Guard. We read you loud and clear, over."

Tuck keyed the mike again, "Charleston Coast Guard, this is the sailing vessel Night Wind. We are departing McClellanville with three crew members and an ETA in Fort Lauderdale, Florida in approximately three days, over."

"Roger, Night Wind, have a safe trip. Charleston Coast Guard out."

Tuck took the radio from its bracket and then stepped outside of the aft cabin where he threw it over the side before returning to the helm.

The ocean was still running three to five feet out of the Southeast, so Tuck set the autopilot for a heading of 150 degrees to take the sea head on, a very comfortable ride at the slow speed that the Perkins afforded. Tuck then went below deck to check on his unwilling passenger.

"Enjoying the trip so far, George?" Tuck asked as he unceremoniously ripped the duct tape off Withers' mouth.

"Are you going to kill me or talk me to death, Tucker?" Withers asked sarcastically.

"Neither actually, George; I found two pounds of Semtex with a cell phone detonator directly under where you are sitting, and a GPS tracker hidden in the electronics. If you can't get free in a couple of hours, I think that your old employers are going to do that for me," Tuck replied with a humorless grin, "Are you feeling all right, George? You are looking a little green."

Withers was getting sea sick, and with his head taped in position, there wasn't anything that he could do about it. Suddenly the urge to vomit overcame him.

"Well, I'm going to leave you with that, George. Good luck on the rest of your voyage," Tuck said as he climbed the companionway to the main cabin. He re-checked the auto steerage and made certain that the vessel was still on course, and then made his way to the aft rail, and the line that towed the Carib dingy. Tuck pulled the dingy alongside the port rail in the lee of the boat and climbed aboard. Once safely at the tiller, he let go of the bowline and drifted free of the Night Wind, which motored sedately away, leaving Tuck and the small inflatable in a very uncomfortable sea. Tuck pulled the rope starter on the fifteen horsepower Tohatsu outboard, and it fired on the first pull, much to his relief. Now would come the most dangerous part of the trip, which was navigating the eleven-foot dingy back several miles to the inlet in a choppy sea…and without being seen.

George Withers was violently sick, but he realized that his only chance of survival was to escape the restraints and get the 'Night Wind' turned back toward land before it reached the unknown coordinates where the planned detonation of the Semtech would take place.

The rising and falling of the yacht's bow was growing more pronounced as it reached deeper water and heavier seas. Suddenly Withers heard something fall and break behind him, and a shard of glass rolled against his hands. Feverishly, he maneuvered the broken glass so that he could saw at the restraining plastic ties, but the blood had left his fingers, and it was almost impossible to tell how much headway he was making or where he was cutting, although he knew from the slippery feel that he had done some damage to his hands and wrists in the attempt. After almost two hours, the plastic finally yielded to the glass dragging against it, and Withers was able to get his arms in the front of him and work at the duct tape that held his head and body to the mast.

As soon as his feet were free, he turned to the task of finding and defusing the explosive device by pulling up the floorboards covering the shallow bilge. There, directly under him just as Tuck had said, was the Semtech and the detonator. Withers carefully, but quickly, defused the device and then climbed the companionway to the aft cabin to take control of the boat. His first view was out the starboard side of the cabin at the graying weather and rolling sea. As he turned to his left to take the wheel, he looked out the port side window of the cabin where his view was blocked by the towering bow of the Greenline container vessel, 'Winter Green' which measured 900 feet in length and over 90 feet in width, sailing from Baltimore, Maryland to Charleston, South Carolina at a speed of twenty-two knots with over forty-eight feet of draft. It was the last thing that George Withers saw as the bow slammed the sailboat just forward of amidships and rolled the yacht over in two shattered pieces, scattering debris along both sides of the ship as it thundered over the hapless smaller vessel.

The last conscious thought of George Withers was the huge screw chopping the stern section of the Night Wind to shreds, and blending him into the wreckage of the aft cabin, which sank slowly to the bottom in twenty fathoms of water.

The five-foot waves coming at the stern of the little rubber dingy gave Tuck a fit as the boat was being slammed side to every time one would smash into him. His visibility from the low vantage point was also suffering so Tuck kept his head down and concentrated on following his compass on a reciprocal course that the Night Wind had followed on the voyage out. Even though he couldn't see land, Tuck knew that keeping the southeasterly wind to his back would put him back on land eventually, but exactly where was going to be a problem. As the next wave overtook the boat, Tuck increased the throttle so that he could ride the top of the wave and gain a small height advantage for a quick look around. All that he could see was what looked like endless ocean and the clouds of an afternoon front moving offshore.

"Great!" thought Tuck dismally, "All I need now is a bigger wind blowing me back offshore."

He knew that there was no way for him to make any speed in the headwind that might possibly be generated by the front, but there was the slight hope that an offshore blow would flatten the ocean out long enough for him to make a run further inshore.

As soon as the thought finished, the southerly wind died down, and the ocean began to flatten. Tuck twisted the throttle and the fifteen horsepower Tohatsu soon had the dingy jumping the smaller waves at close to twenty knots. Tuck held his course and bent forward in the boat while holding the tiller throttle with his left hand. His only hope was to make a few more miles to the rendezvous before the wind picked up into a Nor'easter, which would really slop the ocean up.

The spray off the bow was blowing back into Tuck's face as he buried his head and spoke encouragement to the little outboard,

"Come on Baby, just a few more miles. I know that you've got it in you," then, "Dear Lord, please help us make it in."

As Tuck finished his prayer, the motor coughed twice and shut down. Tuck turned and pulled the starter rope to no avail. He then shook the small gas can and found that it was empty. The one detail that could have guaranteed a safe trip home had been overlooked! His thoughts turned to Hanna and the baby, "Lord, if I don't make it back tonight, please take care of Hanna for me. She is going to need a lot of help."

The sound of a boat horn interrupted Tuck's prayer as an old wooden shrimp boat with Shaun O'Brien at the helm and Bob Pike on deck came up from behind to take him onboard.

"Hey boy," Bob called out, "you flew right past us back there about a mile. If you hadn't stopped, we would never have caught you!"

"Man, am I glad to see you!" Tuck exclaimed in relief, "Is everything worked out?"

Bob helped Tuck pull the boat alongside the shrimp boat while Tuck pulled his pocketknife out and proceeded to shred the stern section of the flotation compartments. He then hurriedly climbed aboard the shrimper before turning to slice into the front and sides of the boat as Bob pulled the bow clear of the water. They both breathed a sigh of relief when the little craft slipped silently below the surface, dragged down by the weight of the motor.

"Shaun, where did you find this old tub?" Tuck asked jokingly as O'Brien set a course back to McClellanville through Price Inlet.

"I talked one of the old shrimp boat captains into renting it to me for a few hours. They don't have any income down here since 85% of our shrimp is now imported from Thailand, so he was anxious to make some extra money. You don't need to worry about who he thinks rented the boat; I used a false identity for that, courtesy of Anthony Morris."

Then Bob called out with relief in his voice, "There's the inlet off the starboard bow!"

The thirty-minute run back to the dock seemed like hours to Tuck. At any minute, he expected to see a law enforcement vessel with lights and sirens running them down, but the trip was fast and uneventful. Hanna was waiting in a whale-sized old Buick station wagon when they docked.

Tuck and Bob left Shaun and the old shrimp boat and jogged to where the car was parked. Hanna got out and gave Tuck a big hug as if she was afraid that he wasn't coming back, which she had been. All that was left to do was to report the Night Wind stolen, as a precaution, and then they could continue on their journey, which now was going to end in Odessa, Texas.

"Hanna, did you get my rucksack packed?" Tuck asked.

"It's in the back on the top. I thought that you might need it before we left," Hanna replied.

Tuck pull the rucksack out of the Buick and dug for the cell phones that he had thrown in the night before. The first call was to the local police who arrived in the form of a sheriff's deputy, and the next was to Special Agent Morris to let him know that George Withers was at sea for a few hours and that they should be able to locate him without too much trouble.

"Tuck there is something else that you should know. We have lost contact with agent Douglas Kensey who we believe may have orchestrated Harry's death, although we still do not have conclusive proof. This man is psychotic and very dangerous, and we are doing what we can to find him," Special Agent Morris confided.

"I understand about Kensey, Agent Morris. We are going dark for a while after this call. If anything comes up, please let Henry Albright know. He can get in touch with us. Thanks for everything you've done," Tuck replied and then ended the call.

"Good news, Tuck?" Bob asked.

"Not quite. It appears that we have another psycho to worry about, but I'm not telling Hanna," Tuck said in a low voice so that she wouldn't hear.

"Well, I've got a small change in plans also," Bob replied to the not so good news, "I'm hitching a ride back to Honduras with Shaun, so we can say our good-byes here, and you guys can get on the road," Bob broke his news solemnly.

"Well, Bob, God speed to you and Shaun. I hope that you and Abigail keep yourselves out of trouble down there in your tropical paradise," Tuck said with a smile as he gave his old friend a big hug.

"Tuck, if this Texas trip doesn't work out, I want you and Hanna to get your butts to Honduras pronto. Do I make myself clear?" Bob scolded Tuck with a smile breaking over his features.

"You do indeed, Bob. If anything goes wrong, we'll be knocking at your door," Tuck promised, although he knew that he probably wouldn't ever get to Honduras if things went wrong.

Bob walked to the beat up pickup with the old fisherman at the wheel and got in. The driver gave a blast on the truck horn and waved good-bye to Tuck and Hanna as he drove out of the marina. Tuck felt a little empty as he watched his friends leave, but his plans revolved around keeping his wife and baby safe, so any other thoughts had to be contained in the compartment that Tuck's mind reserved for unnecessary feelings.

The Deputy finished his report to the Coast Guard and motioned Tuck over.

"Here is your report Mr. Tucker," he said while handing Tuck several pieces of paper and his card, "If anything comes up, we'll give you a call."

"Thank you, sir, should I go ahead and call my insurance about this theft?" Tuck asked innocently.

"I would report it to them Mr. Tucker, but we will probably have your boat back in a few hours. It couldn't have gotten very far," The deputy replied.

Tuck thought to himself, "I hope it got far enough for the Semtech to ignite," and then out loud, "I understand sir; I hope that you can find it quickly. We are supposed to finish our trip before the baby is born."

"We'll do our best," The deputy dismissed Tuck and walked back to his patrol car.

Tuck walked to where Hanna had parked the station wagon out of sight and got in.

"It's time to drive, baby. Let's hit I-95 to Jacksonville and then we'll take I-10 to Texas!" Tuck said as he buckled up.

"Aye aye, Captain," Hanna replied, and pulled the big boat of a car out of the marina and drove toward the main highway.

CHAPTER 36

"Hanna, do you want me to drive yet?" Tuck asked as he noticed Hanna's eyes seemed to be staring out the front window.

"Tuck, I am so tired all of a sudden. Can we stop for the night in Savannah? We're only fifty miles away and I could really use some sleep," Hanna replied.

"Of course, we can Babe. We don't have to be in a hurry to do anything now," Tuck said as if it were true, "There is a rest area up there, pull in and let me drive to a motel."

Hanna pulled the car into the rest area and Tuck waited for her to go the restroom. They were soon back on the road, and as they were nearing Savannah, Georgia Tuck saw a La Quinta Inn that had a vacancy sign. They made the next exit and backtracked down the service road to the motel. After checking in under their fake names, Tuck left Hanna and walked over to a Burger King to get them something to eat. As he was waiting in line, a big screen TV on the sidewall caught his attention. What appeared on the screen next made his legs buckle.

"The Coast Guard has just released these pictures of the container vessel Wintergreen as it pulled into Charleston harbor tonight. If you look closely at the bulbous nose of the ship's bow, you can see the cables and the mast of a sailing vessel that apparently has been run over and sunk by the ship. The captain reported the collision earlier this afternoon just south of Cape Romain, and the Coast guard has deployed their air and sea rescue craft to the area to search for the wreckage. They are speculating that this may have been the yacht 'Night Wind' that was stolen earlier in the afternoon from the dock at McClellanville. We'll keep you updated as this story breaks."

Tuck got his order and jogged back to the room to tell Hanna, but she had already seen the same report that he did.

"Michael, did you have anything to do with this?" she asked suspiciously.

"I swear that I didn't, Hanna. That boat was running fine when I got off," Tuck declared.

"I believe you Michael, but what if Withers got away again?" Hanna sounded worried.

"I don't believe that he could have made it, Hanna. Now let's eat," Tuck said as he divvied up the food, including two chocolate milkshakes.

As they were eating, Hanna started talking about the boat and the insurance money that they would have to collect if it was the one that had been hit, or if it simply disappeared.

"Hon, we can't use our cell phones again until we are settled in Texas. The insurance adjuster will just have to wait a bit, that's all," Tuck reassured her.

"I understand, Michael, but it is a lot of money that we are talking about, almost enough to buy us another house," Hanna persisted.

"If it will make you feel any better, I will call them after we've been in Odessa for two weeks. We can say that we took another type of vacation and didn't check the news. Besides, Anthony Morris will run interference for us if we need him to," Tuck replied.

"Okay, Michael. As long as we don't get into any trouble, you handle it your way," Hanna relented.

They finished their small meal and went to bed early. Hanna slept like a log, but Tuck lay awake most of the night planning his trip. It seemed as if he had only slept for an hour when he was awakened by Hanna shaking his shoulder.

"Come on sleepy head. It is six o'clock and we need to get on the road," she said.

"Let me take a shower, and we'll see if they have any coffee in the lobby," Tuck said groggily.

"I've already got it and two donuts, big boy. Now get your butt out of bed!" Hanna said with a giggle.

"Slave driver!" Tuck muttered under his breath, but he rolled out of bed and hit the shower.

Hanna had the car packed when he got out, so he grabbed the lukewarm Styrofoam cup of coffee and the last donut before heading out behind her.

"I'll drive the first leg," he announced as they got into the car.

"That's fine, Michael. I wanted to look at the maps that I picked up this morning to kind of orient myself a bit," Hanna said with a smile.

"Am I going to have to put up with this joy, joy, joy person all day?" Tuck asked jokingly.

"You'd better be glad that I feel this good, Mr. Tucker, it might not last forever. I am pregnant and moody, as you well know," Hanna laughed, "Let's get down the road a bit and find a real restaurant to eat breakfast in."

"Already ahead of you, Mrs. Tucker, I'm stopping at the first Cracker Barrel that I see," Tuck announced knowing that a Cracker Barrel Restaurant was Hanna's favorite place to eat.

CHAPTER 37

The April sun was high overhead and the temperature was hitting eighty degrees when Tuck and Hanna reached Odessa, and their exit onto FM1936 off I-20. It had been close to six hours since they left Dallas with no air conditioner in the old station wagon, and Hanna was miserable.

"How much longer, Michael?" She asked with a noticeable strain in her voice.

"We've probably got less than half an hour, Babe, just hold on. I've got to call Mr. Post and let him know where we are. He is supposed to meet us at the ranch gate and lead us in," Tuck answered as he made the call.

"I just want to lay down somewhere cool and rest my back. The baby is almost as cranky as I am," Hanna tried to sound light, but three days on the road had taken their toll on her. It was time for a rest, both emotionally and physically.

"Hello Mr. Post, this is Michael Tucker," A brief silence followed, then, "Okay, John it is. We are just getting on FM1936, and you told me to call for directions from here," Tuck carried on the conversation with John Post, the Manager of the big ranch that Uncle Henry had made the arrangement with.

Hanna just looked out of the window at the oil rigs and pump jacks that seemed to be growing out of the mesquite scrub and cactus of the surrounding flat country.

Tuck drove until he came to the Kermit Highway and turned left toward Goldsmith.

"It won't be long now Hanna. John said it was about three miles down this road, and he would be on the right in a big pickup truck."

"Michael just look at all of this space and all of those oil wells. Have you ever seen anything like it?" Hanna asked.

"Well, Afghanistan was a big place with a lot of desert, but it didn't look like this. I kind of like this place, what do you think?" Tuck asked her in hopes that Hanna would perk up a little before they met John.

Hanna gave him a tired smile, "It's a big change from South Carolina, but I suppose it will grow on me, Mr. Tucker."

John Post was sitting on the tailgate of the ranch truck in front of a big set of red pipe gates. He saw the old station wagon coming and waved his work hat to get Tuck's attention.

"There it is Hanna, our new home for a while!" Tuck exclaimed excitedly as he pulled in behind the truck and got out to meet their host. Hanna watched them shake hands and saw John turn to look at her. She waved and gave him her best smile as Tuck returned to the car.

"We are going to follow him to the house. Mrs. Post is waiting for us," Tuck said to Hanna as he drove through the gate behind John.

The heavy steel gate slid shut behind them, and they drove in the dust of the pickup for what seemed like three or four miles down a rough dirt road, and past several big oil rigs that were busy drilling for the precious liquid and gas that had made this part of the country pretty independent.

After about ten minutes of driving the rough roads and dodging the occasional cow or bull, they pulled into what seemed to be an oasis with a small stone house, surrounded by stately cottonwood trees, and a large pond full of geese. Coming out of the gate was a lady that could only have been Mrs. Post. She was in her mid-sixties, but looked much younger due in large part to the hard work of managing the ranch with her husband, and living in the tranquil environment that the secluded area offered.

Hanna got out of the car slowly and walked around to meet John and Mary Louise Post. John shook Hanna's hand first and introduced himself, and then said to Hanna, "This is my wife, Mary Louise."

"Hanna. What a lovely name," Mary Louise said while taking Hanna's hand and flashing a big Texas smile, "I'm so happy that you and your husband could come and stay with us. I get so few visitors out here anymore. Let's go inside and get you off your feet for a bit. When you have rested, I'll show you the guest house," Mary Louise said referring to the smallish two bedroom stone bunkhouse that stood behind the ranch house, "You men get the car unloaded while Miss Hanna and I get to know each other."

"Well, I guess that is our queue, Michael. It is Michael right?" John asked politely.

"My friends call me Tuck," Tuck answered.

"Tuck it is then. Henry told me about some of that mess that you were in back east. We could use some of your talents right here if you don't mind hunting a few pesky coyotes and the occasional cougar for me."

"I'd love to help in any way that I can," Tuck replied.

"Good. I know you and the Missus are tired and need to relax so let's go over to the bunkhouse and get you settled in. There'll be plenty of time for talkin' afterwards," John said as he led the way to the bunkhouse.

The Posts invited Tuck and Hanna for dinner that evening and regaled them with stories about west Texas ranch life. It was then that Tuck learned that the ranch was about two hundred and forty thousand acres broken down into one mile square 'sections', with each section being six hundred and forty acres, and that a couple of the several ponds, or tanks as they were called, had been home to several large alligators that had been turned loose on a whim almost thirty years before. John pointed out a windmill about a half of a mile from the house.

"Right behind that windmill, there is a tank with two big 'gators in it. We feed them coyote parts and any of the cows or deer that get killed out here. One of them is around eleven feet long, and the female is not much smaller," He said while pointing off in the general direction of the tank.

"You've got to be kidding me, John. How in the world would an alligator get to the desert in West Texas?" Tuck asked incredulously.

They used to sell them at Wacker's five and dime about thirty or so years ago, and many of the ranchers brought them home to their kids who eventually put them in the water tanks. We had all three gators in that pond out back until a few years before I took over here. The fellow before me took them out and put them in that tank that I showed you, and they got pretty big on all of the coyotes and other stuff that were fed to them over the years," John replied.

Tuck was fascinated and would have asked questions all night if Hanna had not taken him gently by the arm and tugged him toward the door.

"I really need to lie down, dear, and we have taken up too much of these good people's time," She said sweetly before hugging Mary Louise good night.

Tuck shook John's hand and asked, "Can I jog over to the tank in the morning?"

"Sure Tuck, just follow that road until you get to the power line right-of-way, turn right and follow the wires to the tank. Watch out for snakes and any of the bulls that might be out there. You never know about their disposition. You kids have a quiet night, and we'll see you in the morning," John gave them a big smile as they walked to the little house.

"Mary Lou, I hope these kids can relax here. From what Henry told me, they've had it rough."

She just squeezed his hand and said, "They're survivors, John. Hanna reminds me of myself when I was her age."

John just smiled as he gave her a hug and walked back into the house.

The days turned into three weeks with Tuck in his routine, and Hanna looking better than she had looked in months. Every morning Tuck was up before daylight, slipping out of the house without waking Hanna, and making the run to the water tank. Once there, he took a big drink of water from the pipe on the old windmill that fed the concrete holding tank, which in turn overflowed into the pond. After a drink of cool, sweet water, he would walk to the pond edge and just stare at the big 'gator that he had nicknamed 'Big Joe', and then he would turn and run back home, arriving just in time for one of Hanna's breakfasts. After breakfast, he would accompany John on his rounds and then spend the evening calling predators on various areas of the ranch.

This morning was different somehow. That feeling that something was not quite right was on him, and no matter how hard he tried to dismiss it, the feeling that something was wrong kept coming back stronger than ever.

It had taken Douglas Kensey two weeks to discover Michael Tucker's location in Goldsmith, Texas. Tuck had finally contacted his insurance carrier to settle the unfinished business of the lost yacht, and a red flag was raised which led directly to Tuck's location on the ranch. Kensey intercepted that information through an old and trusted informant, and now he was in a position to kill Michael Tucker. In Kensey's deluded mind, Tuck represented the reason for his descent into obscurity that had started with the fiasco in Honduras. Everything that Douglas Kensey had worked so hard for was erased in the several weeks of hospital confinement and punishing interrogation sessions that followed his attempt on Abigail Pike. His successful, and impossible to prove, murder of Harry Albright fueled his pathetic ego, and now that he had studied Tuck's early morning routine for the past week, Kensey decided that this was the morning Michael Tucker would die.

He packed in undetected the two miles from the highway a good two hours before daybreak and set up at the edge of the pond with a good view of the road just beyond the holding tank where Tuck was certain to stop for his morning drink. The Remington M-24 rested on a short bipod with the muzzle pointed in the general direction of the tank. Kensey knew that he was over gunned for the seventy-yard shot that he would make to even the score with Tucker, but he wanted to make certain of a one shot kill. An added plus would be seeing Tucker's face as the bullet ripped the life out of him. At the thought, Kensey's face broke into a grin as he settled himself into position and racked a round into the chamber of his rifle. With the safety on and his finger just brushing the light trigger in a lover's caress, he waited for Tuck to appear.

Tuck heard his own feet pounding the hard packed dirt of the road in a steady rhythm and increased his pace. He could feel the power returning to his legs after weeks of not training, and he felt more alive than he had in ages. Tuck jumped the fence in one fluid move as he turned onto the power line right-of-way and saw the high ground of the water tank ahead on his left. Soon the bank was on his immediate left and the windmill in sight, so Tuck increased his pace to a sprint. The burning in his lungs told him to pull back a bit, but Tuck knew his body, and he willed his legs to push even harder as he flew across the hard packed earth. He made the turn down the path to the tank and slowed slightly to cool down before stopping for his drink.

As he slowed to a walk about twenty yards from the concrete holding tank, Tuck saw a large splash in the distance, close to the edge of the pond. His curiosity aroused, Tuck scooped a handful of water from the end of the discharge pipe and walked to the pond.

The water was roiled and muddy indicating that Big Joe had taken something large very close to the water's edge. As Tuck got closer, the first thing that he spotted was a shooter's mat and drag bag lying close to the pond. Then he saw drag marks and blood leading into the pond, and about five feet from the water's edge, the barrel of an M-24 rifle sticking up about six inches above the muddy water. Looking closer at the drag marks, Tuck saw the unmistakable claw marks of a human hand as it tried desperately, but in vain, to gain a hold in the hard earth of the pond's edge, and two deep lines that had been cut by the bipod of the M-24 rifle as it was drug backwards into the pond.

The ringing of his cell phone startled Tuck, "Hello?" He answered slowly as he looked around his location.

"Michael Tucker, you need to get home now, Michael Junior is on the way!" Mary Louise's voice stressed the urgency of Hanna's situation, "John is on the way to pick you up. Please hurry!"

"I'll be there in a few minutes, Ma'am!" Tuck exclaimed and ended the call.

He stood there for a moment while the understanding of the situation slowly came to him before turning to pick up a length of pipe that had been left near the pond, which he calmly used to push the rifle barrel underwater and out of sight.

Not surprising to Tuck, any reservations that he might have had about not reporting this had completely disappeared.

As he started the run back to his beloved Hanna, he heard Harry's voice say, "The Lord works in mysterious ways Son."

"Yes, He does, Harry. Yes, He certainly does!"

The End

Acknowledgements

Once again, my heartfelt thanks to all of my friends and family members that contributed to this endeavor, especially to my brother Stuart Dallas for his encouragement and reading skills, and Tom Stewart, the Texan who inspired the ending of the book. Thanks also to George and Lou Etta Shackelford for their hospitality at the 'T' Ranch.

Thank you also to Bob Holliday for his encouragement, and for his sighting of the big cougar leaving the swamp above Myrtle Beach shortly after we published the first book.

I want to thank the local establishments that are mentioned in the book for allowing me to use them for 'local flavor', and to the manufacturers and marketers of the various equipment and clothing mentioned that have also lent a sense of realism to this purely fictional work.

R.I.P

Weston, our beloved yellow lab that played the part of 'Weston' in the novel 'COUGAR!', and in this sequel, was killed last year by a hit and run driver. I hope that they have a few squirrels wherever good dogs end up.

W.W. Brock